Th

From

The Kinley company   d in British fashion for more than a century, but a series of bad investments has left the coffers nearly bare and the company in need of a miracle.

Now, to right the wrongs of their parents and save the Kinley name and legacy, the estranged Kinley siblings—Jonathan, Olivia and Caleb—will have to set aside their differences to come together and show the world what "family" really means.

Escape to the Cotswolds in Jonathan's story:
Reunion with the Brooding Millionaire

Follow Olivia's story in London and Paris:
Rules of Their Parisian Fling

Both available now!

And prepare to embark on a vacation in
Lake Como in Caleb's story
Coming soon from Harlequin Romance!

Dear Reader,

Welcome back to The Kinley Legacy! If you're new to this wonderfully chaotic family, where bickering and sibling affection are entirely indistinguishable, welcome! You're going to have so much fun here.

I've adored Livia Kinley ever since she made such an impact in the first book in this series and I spent a month trying to tease her out of it. Given her own book, she has run riot. Adam Jackson is the only person who can possibly keep her in line, and it was such a pleasure making him a man who was worthy of Liv.

I hope you enjoy their story as much as I enjoyed writing it.

Love,

Ellie Darkins

Rules of Their Parisian Fling

Ellie Darkins

HARLEQUIN
Romance

Recycling programs
for this product may
not exist in your area.

ISBN-13: 978-1-335-40717-7

Rules of Their Parisian Fling

Harlequin Enterprises ULC
22 Adelaide St. West, 41st Floor
Toronto, Ontario M5H 4E3, Canada
www.Harlequin.com

Printed in U.S.A.

Ellie Darkins spent her formative years devouring romance novels and after completing her English degree, decided to make a living from her love of books. As a writer and editor, she finds her work now entails dreaming up romantic proposals, hot dates with alpha males and trips to the past with dashing heroes. When she's not working, she can usually be found running around after her toddler, volunteering at her local library, or escaping all the above with a good book and a vanilla latte.

Books by Ellie Darkins

Harlequin Romance

Newborn on Her Doorstep
Holiday with the Mystery Italian
Falling for the Rebel Princess
Conveniently Engaged to the Boss
Surprise Baby for the Heir
Falling Again for Her Island Fling
Reunited by the Tycoon's Twins
Snowbound at the Manor
From Best Friend to Fiancée
Prince's Christmas Baby Surprise
Reunion with the Brooding Millionaire

Visit the Author Profile page at Harlequin.com.

Praise for
Ellie Darkins

CHAPTER ONE

'Ah, here she is. Livia, I'd like you to meet Adam Jackson.'

Livia frowned, her brother's introduction and the man's name not giving her any clue who this stranger in her office was or what he was doing there. She turned to look at him, her eyebrows raised, waiting for the pair of them to fill her in. He was hardly an unwelcome addition to the décor, she had to concede. Tall, dark-haired and handsome, he was a walking cliche, and she offered him her hand, wishing that she wasn't meeting him at work, and wondering whether she was going to have the chance to get to know him better. His thoughts had clearly gone somewhere similar. She watched the widening of his eyes and the slight pinking of his lightly tanned white skin and knew that her interest was very much mutual.

'Adam is a management consultant specialising in the luxury beauty industry,' her brother said. 'I've hired him to work with you on the fragrance project.'

Livia's brows raised further as she fought the urge to snap. What on earth was her brother playing at? But that wouldn't exactly be professional, and she didn't want to spoil the mutual ogle that she had going on with this guy she was about to eject from the building. So she turned to her brother and smiled, trying to keep her voice smooth. 'Is there a reason you think that I can't handle it myself?'

Jonathan shook his head. 'I think you're perfectly competent,' he said, his voice as carefully controlled as hers. 'But this is an ambitious project and I don't want you to be overstretched. Don't think I haven't noticed how many hours you've been putting in recently.'

She turned to the man standing beside her brother, cursing the universe for providing such a crushable item, and then immediately snatching it away from her. 'Adam, I'm so sorry you've had a wasted journey but there is no position available on my team.' She headed for the door to show them out, with just a touch of regret, but her brother was taller than her and beat her to it, with Adam not far behind. She crossed her arms, waiting for the pair of them to move.

'I tried to tell you last week,' Jonathan said. 'I requested a meeting and you said you had no time, if you remember?'

'I prioritised a meeting with Claude Gaspard. If I'd known that you were going to go over my head to do this, I would have made the time,' she explained.

'Liv, it's not like that,' Jonathan said gently, which pushed her blood pressure just that little bit higher. 'We all want this to be a success, but not at any cost. You're working yourself too hard and you need someone who can share the load.'

'Oh, and you just assume that I'm not capable—?'

She was interrupted then by a very unsubtle clearing of a throat to her left. She glanced across at him, remembered how pretty he was and fixed her eyes back on Jonathan, cursing the universe once again.

'I'm sorry, Adam,' Jonathan said, seeming to remember that they weren't alone.

'Liv, we'll talk about this more later. For now, find a way to work with Adam because he's staying. Adam, come see me before you leave for the day and we'll talk about that other thing.'

And with that, her brother left them alone. She knew that her anger shouldn't be directed at Adam. It should be directed at her overbearing older brother who had been a stand-in dad since their parents had abandoned them when she was a teenager. But she couldn't be mad at him, because he was only doing it because he loved her. He was marrying her best friend, and he'd just walked out of the room anyway. Or she could be mad at the universe for showing her something that she wanted, but she couldn't have. So she turned all that on Adam.

She'd betrayed herself a dozen times over in her mind—her imagination was a quick worker, and his tight T-shirt and muscled arms provided plenty of fantasy material—but she forced the thoughts out of her mind as she turned to face him.

'Adam. I'm sorry that my brother has got ahead of himself—'

But Adam folded his arms, emphasising

the muscles in them, and looking irritatingly unconcerned by the fact that she was trying to fire him.

'Your brother is the CEO,' he said, without a hint of doubt in his voice. 'This is his call.'

'That's a technicality,' Liv replied. 'This is a family business and—'

'Everyone reports to him, don't they?' Adam interrupted. 'Including you. That "technicality" means he signed my contract this morning and there's nothing that you can do about it.' He thought for a moment, his lips pursing slightly in a way that did nothing for her fickle libido. 'Well, you can sue me out of it, I suppose,' he conceded eventually with every appearance of generosity, and a smile that made her want to do bad things. 'If you wanted to, that is. But it would be a waste of your time and money and it sounds like you haven't got a lot of either to spare.'

He was right, she knew. She didn't have time to be distracted by trying to get rid of him. Since she'd finally talked her brother into their family's fashion house launching its own fragrance and cosmetics line, she'd devoted what felt like every waking hour to the project. That was the reason she'd not been able to find time for a meeting with Jonathan when he'd tried to find half an hour in her schedule at the last minute without telling her what it was about.

At the time, she'd been playing phone tag with a master parfumier in Paris who she was trying to convince *did* have space in his schedule this year to recreate the scent that her great-grandmother had developed but never launched in the nineteen-thirties. Her best friend, Rowan, had found the old paperwork in the family's Cotswold manor house in the summer of the previous year. And if Rowan hadn't somehow come out of that weekend having mostly pulled the stick out of Jonathan's backside and making him somewhat human, and then fallen in love and got engaged to him, the project probably would have gone nowhere.

But a lovestruck Jonathan who was marrying her best friend had been more willing to listen to her than he ever had been before. She realised now that she'd been relying on those changes being permanent, rather than a honeymoon period, and it had made her complacent.

'So we'll pay you,' she told Adam, trying to think through the quickest way to get this obstacle out of her path and to keep her project on track. Hoping he wasn't aware that the company didn't have the money to spare for spurious legal cases. 'But I don't need your help. I've been working on this for months and I'm perfectly capable of launching it myself.'

Adam shook his head, not moving from where he appeared to have grown roots right in front of her desk. 'I'm not being paid for a job I didn't do.'

'Then return the money,' she said, trying to make it sound flippant, as if she really didn't care what he did. She flicked through some papers on her desk, trying to look as if she were perfectly collected.

Adam laughed and the sound caught her by surprise, making her look up and stare at him for a long couple of seconds. His face was transformed by it, and for a moment she wondered what it would be like to make him laugh like that without it carrying such a heavy dose of contempt for him. But she fought the thought down. She had no interest in making him laugh—or do anything else, for that matter, other than leave her office.

She saw heat in his expression too, and something more dangerous. Something that told her she couldn't let this desire of hers off the leash for even a second if she didn't want something to happen between them.

'I'm sorry. I don't have time for this. I'm expecting a phone call,' she told him, her eyes anywhere but on him.

'If it's a call about the fragrance project, then I should be on it,' Adam replied, which was not the answer that she had been looking for.

There was no way she was letting that happen. The only slight hitch with that determination was that the call would be coming into her office any minute now, and she wasn't sure how to get a six-foot beefcake out of a room in that sort of timeframe. Right on cue, the phone on her desk rang, and, without breaking eye contact with her, Adam leaned forward and pressed the button that answered the call on speakerphone. She glared at him but there was nothing she could do about it as the line connected to Paris.

'*Bonjour,*' she trilled, trying to keep her irritation out of her voice. She listened to the rapid-fire French at the other end of the line—which would have been a thousand per cent easier if she hadn't been trying to force the fact that Adam was in the room out of her mind at the same moment she 'uh-huh'-and-'*oui*'-ed her way through the call, making none of the carefully considered constructive feedback notes she'd been working on the night before. Which was perfect because now Adam thought that she was incompetent and he and Jonathan could have a good laugh about how useless she was. And then Jonathan would probably work out that she wasn't worth the trouble, push her out of the business and have Adam take over completely.

She got the call over with as quickly as she could, deciding that she should probably quit while she was ahead. Or, at least, before she fell any further behind.

'Are all your calls as pointless as that?' Adam asked, that beautiful mouth turned up in a sneer that made her want to smash a cream pie into it, just to see whether he was capable of any other expression.

'I work better without a guard dog watching over me,' she told him, wondering how long he was planning on standing idly at her desk while she pretended that she was able to get her work done. 'Were you planning on getting out of my office at any point?' she asked in return.

'I don't know. Depends whether you're planning on sharing your diary with me so I can join your meetings.'

She forced out a fake laugh. 'You're going to have to try harder than that if you want to read my diary, Adam.'

He crossed his arms again and stared her down. '*Secret Confessions of a Little Princess*? Thanks, but I think I'll pass.'

'You don't know anything about me.'

'I've seen enough,' he said with a smirk that she assumed was meant to imply that he had met plenty of women just like her—rich and pretty and working for a family business.

Oh, he thought that he knew her. Most likely thought that she only had a job here through nepotism. That she'd been given a position at the family business because that was what families like hers did with girls like her. But he didn't know her. Didn't know how hard she had resisted drawing on her family name or joining the company. How she had spent months preparing business plans, digging through archives and researching her market. Adam might think that he was about to walk in and take the reins from some spoiled little princess who didn't know what she was doing, but he was wrong, and he would have to prise those reins from her cold, dead hands. This project was her passion, and she did not mess about when it came to her passions.

True, she hadn't been at her best on that call just now, but that was entirely Adam's fault. She would have handled it just fine if he hadn't been there looming over her desk in a childish attempt to intimidate her.

'Fine. I'll have my assistant share my schedule with you if it will get you out of my sight. We're done here, Adam.'

Conceding to Adam's demands was really not a precedent that she wanted to set, but she had to come up with a plan for what she was going to do to deal with this completely unwelcome development. She just needed some time to think.

He smirked. Again. And there were a dozen things that she could do to wipe that expression off his face. At least fifty per cent of them would lead to prison time and the rest involved more nudity than was typically wise in one's place of work.

'This conversation isn't over,' he said. But didn't turn for the door. She rolled her eyes and turned back to her desktop monitor, hoping that eventually he'd get tired of trying to stare her down, do her a favour and leave. Eventually she heard his shoes on the carpet, moving towards the door of the office, and as his footsteps faded down the corridor she finally let herself breathe normally.

'Liv, I need you in my office!'

She suppressed a groan at the sound of her brother's voice. It was gone eight o'clock and she was starving. What was more, there would be no escape from him when she got home. Since he'd revealed the money troubles the business was having, they'd all clubbed together to work out the best way to use their assets to provide a cash injection. And right now, that meant that she and her two brothers had all given up their individual homes to live in the house that she had inherited from her grandmother the year before. She'd probably sell it, once they had a minute to think about how to do that, given the amount of paperwork selling a listed building that had been in her family for a hundred years would produce.

'Jonathan, couldn't this wait until we're home?' she said, pushing files into her bag as she walked through the door to her brother's office.

When she looked up, she was half a step from colliding with the broad chest and black T-shirt of Adam Jackson.

'Oh, of course you're here,' she groaned, earning her a smirk from Adam and a tired sigh from Jonathan. At least she would be home soon, where—with Rowan or alone— she could lock herself in her room and pretend that her brother didn't exist. 'Jonathan, can't we do this at home? It's late, and I'm sure you want to get back to Rowan.' It was a cheap shot, but she wasn't above taking advantage of her brother's one soft spot. Not after the day that she'd just had. Jonathan's face melted, until he caught himself and scowled, realising what she'd just done.

'We need to do it now,' he told her. 'Because it's *about* home. Adam's moved down from Scotland to take up this position, and the hotel he booked has just called to cancel his reservation. I've invited him to stay at the house.'

Livia gaped at her brother. He couldn't seriously be dropping this on her now, with no warning. 'At *the* house? At *my* house, you mean.' She knew that she sounded childish. And spoiled. And everything that she had wanted to prove to Adam that she was not.

'I thought we were all okay with inviting people to stay in our homes,' Jonathan said, with a show of wide-eyed innocence. Which would have been fair, if she'd been in a mood to acknowledge it, given that she'd been the one to invite Rowan on their trip to his house the year before, not able to face the thought of spending the week with her brothers without the back-up of her best friend.

She shouldn't have been surprised, really, how spectacularly that had backfired. Now she couldn't even depend on her best friend to always take her side. They tried their hardest to never mention the elephant in the room, because she couldn't bear the thought that if it came down to it, Rowan would choose Jonathan over her.

She didn't need a therapist to tell her that her parents' flight to South America to avoid tax evasion charges made her paranoid that people were going to leave her—though several therapists had told her exactly that, of course. None of The Work that she'd done in her very expensive therapy had managed to stop her believing that they wouldn't have gone if they'd loved her a little more, if she had been a little more loveable. It had seemed easier since she'd decided that she would simply not make herself available for getting hurt. It was too late to not love Rowan. She had been her best friend for years and would be her sister soon too. But that was it. She was officially bolting the stable door. No more people in her life. No one who could leave her. No one she could lose. So their domestic situation was already loaded with enough emotion without this irritating man crashing.

'No, Jonathan, absolutely not,' she told him.

'I wasn't asking your permission. You set the precedent last year,' he said, taking the high-handed headmaster tone that she hated so much. God, it was so annoying when he used her own behaviour against her.

'This is not the same,' she said with forced politeness. 'I invited *Rowan*,' she reminded him. 'Who we had both known for years. Who you were already half in love with. Not some strange man who might murder me in my sleep!'

She thought she heard Adam suppress a laugh and didn't trust herself to look at him.

'If it helps,' Adam offered, with a hint of amusement in his voice that made her see red, and also clench her thighs just a little, 'I really don't have any interest in murdering you. In your sleep or otherwise.'

If only that feeling were mutual. She took a deep breath, reminded herself that she was at work, and was a professional, and losing her temper at Adam would only be handing Jonathan a stick to beat her with.

'It doesn't help, and this is actually a private conversation, so why don't you just wait outside, Adam?'

CHAPTER TWO

ADAM WAITED OUTSIDE the office, though he wasn't sure why they'd bothered to chuck him out when they were first going to raise their voices so half the building could have heard them if they hadn't been the only people still in the office long after everyone else had left to have a social life, or a personal life, or any sort of a life that didn't revolve around their job.

He didn't envy them. He'd made his work his whole life and had never regretted it. It had started from necessity—when you started with nothing you worked every hour of the day or risked spending the rest of your life with nothing. Somewhere along the line it had stopped being something he did and just became who he was. If he stopped, if he risked his life taking a backwards slide… He knew what abject poverty felt like—the constant aching grind of going to bed, night after night, cold and hungry. And then the years when even a bed wasn't a given and he and his mother had surfed from sofa to sofa, until he'd left school and got his first job and between them they'd finally scraped enough money together for a deposit on a tiny flat. From then on, his only focus had been keeping that roof over their heads. And the day that he'd bought a house had felt like the first day of his life he'd taken a truly deep breath. And the next day? He'd been back in the office at six.

While the little princess currently yelling at her brother on the other side of this insufficiently sound-proofed door might have been the most adorably pint-sized piece of perfection he'd seen in a really long time, he had no patience for her. Having her little tantrum because there was going to be one less spare room in the mansion she got to live in rent-free. He'd already booked a hotel for this week while he tried to find a place to buy now that he was back in London. But when they'd called to say that they'd cocked it up and Jonathan had offered him a room, he had agreed. Old habits died hard, after all, and the hotel hadn't been cheap.

The shouting from the office had stopped, and he leaned against the assistant's desk directly in front of the door. The tense silence in the air was every bit as voluble as the shouting had been.

Livia exited the office first, stalking out of the room with her face thunderous and her arms folded. The tense line of her jaw had done something that made her cheekbones pop, and her lips were pursed into a lush pout. Her eyeliner hadn't quite lasted the day and the smudge under her lower lashes gave her a hard-edged look. The overall effect was… Well, it was devastating, wasn't it? And there was no point trying to deny what he wanted, because seeing it for what it was would help him to focus on all the reasons why he didn't want her. She was spoiled. And entitled. And had hated him almost on sight, which helped. Only, that 'almost' was doing a lot of work. Because he couldn't quite make his brain forget those seconds before Jonathan had introduced him properly when her eyes had raked over him as if she'd wanted to follow them with her nails.

They'd started on his face—eyes, jaw, chin. Across his shoulders and down his chest. Slowing down over his belly, until her eyes had flared and she'd shaken her gaze loose somewhere around his thighs. He'd had the ridiculous urge to flex for her, even though she represented everything he hated.

'You finished?' he asked as the yelling seemed to have been replaced by a stony silence.

'There's no need to look so smug about it,' she replied.

Her privileged life made a mockery of the years, decades, of work that he'd put in to become her social and business equal. She'd been planning on helping herself to him too, he was sure, until she'd discovered he'd been brought in to do the actual work on her little pet project.

And if he'd had any doubts about how much his help was needed, listening in on her phone call had been enough to dispel them. She'd been flustered and unfocussed and he'd had no qualms about pointing that out to her. The sooner she accepted that she needed his help and let him do his job, the better.

She pushed past him, her shoulder giving him a little shove even though there was plenty of space between the desks, and he suppressed a little smile at her show of defiance. A tiny, tiny part of him—which he absolutely wasn't going to indulge—got off on the fact that she couldn't hide her reaction to him, even the urge to give him a shove like a kid in a playground. Fine. Good. He wanted her hostile to him, angry.

And if she wanted to find excuses for her body to knock into his, he wasn't going to complain.

'Careful there,' he said, and smiled at the glare she sent in his direction. Her being angry with him was safer anyway, so he wouldn't be tempted by that body and those big sad eyes.

He waited for Jonathan, and they walked down to the parking garage beneath the office building, where Livia was leaning against the hood of a black saloon car.

'I'm driving, she said, holding her hands out to Jonathan for the keys.

'Sure. I'll sit in the back,' Jonathan said. 'Give you two a chance to get to know each other.'

Adam did his best to hide a smile at the absolutely murderous look Livia sent in Jonathan's direction. He shouldn't be enjoying Livia getting riled. He shouldn't be thinking about Livia at all, apart from in a purely professional way.

'What's your next step with Gaspard?' he asked her, wanting to get things back onto a safer professional footing, but she turned that murderous look on him. It was decidedly less enjoyable when he was the victim rather than a bystander.

'I was trying to decide between doing nothing and doing something catastrophically incompetent. Which would you recommend?' she asked sweetly.

Adam decided that grin was getting harder and harder to resist. 'Well, you tried incompetence on the phone today. Perhaps doing nothing would be for the best. Just let me know if you want me to step in.'

She turned a full-watt smile on him, glancing away from the road for a second, and he was momentarily stunned at the sight of it, wondering if she was going to turn sweet, grateful. His imagination was way ahead of him, imagining all the ways that he could enjoy a grateful, pliable Liv.

'You can step in if it's over my rotting, bloated corpse,' she said, her voice still sweet, and with a flirtatious bat of her eyelashes. 'If you're trying to force me out,' she added, 'you're going to have to do a lot more than just ask me nicely.'

He held up his hands. 'I'm not trying to force you anywhere. I just want to see a job done well.'

'And what makes you think that I can't do that? You don't even know me.'

He wondered whether Jonathan was listening from the back seat and wondered about the dynamics in their relationship. He'd read about what had happened with their parents, leaving the country—that was bound to mess a person up. Didn't siblings bond over shared trauma?

He'd always assumed that would have been the case if he'd had any. But then he'd never been able to get his head round companionship versus another mouth to feed. Another bed to find every night. So in the end he'd been glad it was just him and his mum against the world. He tried to picture what their relationship would have looked like if they'd lived the sort of life where houses like this one just dropped into your lap, and he simply…couldn't. Their relationship, for so long, had been about surviving; he didn't know who else they were to one another. Didn't know another way to love.

And when it came to women, sex, relationships—he didn't want to be responsible for anyone else's happiness. It was too much—hurt too much—when you failed someone. He thought about the nights when he hadn't been able to find somewhere for them to stay. When dinner had been a shared Pot Noodle after his mother had finished a twelve-hour shift. How utterly useless he had felt, and how much worse it had been than letting himself down. He had no idea why anyone would willingly seek out more people to be responsible for, to love. Couldn't get his head round there being entire industries built on it. He'd figured out a long time ago that the minute he thought he might have feelings for someone, it was time to walk away. And as long as he found like-minded partners and everyone was upfront about what they wanted, everyone came out of it feeling...fine.

He slid a look sideways at Livia, wondering if she was a like-minded person, or whether she was the 'hearts and flowers and diamond rings' type.

He gave himself a mental slap. Because he didn't care what sort of relationships Liv liked. It did not matter what Livia was into. He wasn't going there. Even without all his usual relationship rules, this would be too complicated. She was too complicated. So he probably shouldn't let his eyes drop to her soft thighs.

The twenty-minute drive dragged, and by the time they pulled up outside the white stucco-fronted town house that could only be described as a mansion Adam could barely suppress his eye roll. Of course their house looked like this. No doubt theirs was still a single residence. He remembered the weeks he had spent in a bedsit, one of six that had been carved out of a building that must have looked just like this one once. He'd lost count of how many people had lived in those six tiny flats, and felt a wave of resentment towards the siblings who were having this whole house land in their laps and didn't even seem to realise how lucky they were.

How did they live with themselves, owning a place like this, when he knew without a doubt there must be people within streets of here experiencing hunger, homelessness and the sort of bone-deep insecurity that he still carried with him years after he'd considered himself successful and financially stable?

'We're here,' Liv said, unbuckling her seat belt and sliding out of the car, evidently not expecting a response. Good, because he doubted that she'd like what he had to say. He followed Jonathan and Livia up the stairs to the glossy black front door, flanked by classical pillars, with his hands clenched into fists and his jaw so tight that he thought he might crack a molar.

'Honey, I'm home,' Liv called out in the grand, checked-floor hallway, and it was enough to distract him momentarily from his anger. He'd just assumed that she was single, but that was ridiculous really, because just look at her. He rapidly readjusted his assumptions when a tall, striking woman appeared on the stairs. But when she kissed

Liv on the cheek and Jonathan on the mouth he guessed that this must be the Rowan he'd heard so much about.

After introductions were made, Rowan and Jonathan disappeared down the stairs to the lower-ground floor—where he guessed the kitchen was located—and left him alone with Liv, who had been given vague instructions to 'get him settled'.

She looked fairly annoyed about it, but didn't say anything, which he guessed was a result of Rowan's influence.

'Come on, then,' Livia said, walking up the grand staircase. He followed her along a long hallway as she pointed out the bedrooms.

'Rowan and Jonathan's room, Caleb's room...' He heard the sound of typing within, and guessed Caleb had locked himself away. He couldn't blame the guy.

'My room,' Livia went on as they reached the end of the corridor. 'This is the only spare room on this floor. It, er, has an interconnecting bathroom with mine. The other bedrooms are in the attic and are usually used for storage, so...'

'This will be fine,' he said, mainly to annoy

her, because he suspected that she'd like nothing more than to send him up to what must have been servants' quarters so he could be neither seen nor heard. Which meant that, as much as he'd prefer to be as far as possible from the ostentatious glamour, and shared bathroom, of the family rooms, he would put up with it if it meant annoying Livia.

CHAPTER THREE

LIVIA SAT AT the kitchen worktop, nursing a sweating glass of Sauvignon Blanc. This was so typical of Jonathan. Inviting someone she was inclined to hate to stay in their house, and then stealing Rowan away with the least subtle, 'We're just going to… ahem…something…ahem…upstairs… ahem…something…' she'd ever heard in her life. And Caleb was showing no signs of suddenly wanting to leave his room and actually spend time with his family. She really would rather be anywhere but here, but her best friend was upstairs being *unsubtle* with Jonathan and there wasn't anyone else she could drag out at a moment's notice as she could with Rowan.

She heard footsteps on the stairs, and, as it was only one set rather than the four-footed

Rowan-Jonathan, she assumed that hunger had tempted Caleb down from his cave.

'Oh. It's you,' she said, surprise forcing the words out of her as Adam appeared in the doorway.

'Do you make all your guests feel so welcome?' he asked with a smirk that irritated her to the tips of her fingers.

'You're Jonathan's guest,' she said with a swig of her wine. 'Nothing to do with me.'

'What is it with you two?' Adam asked, leaning on the marble countertop opposite her and fixing her with a look that on a less detestable man might have done things to her insides. She rolled her eyes.

'Just sibling stuff.' Like trying to be your dad when you really wanted a brother, and stealing your best friend away and making her love him more. But she didn't feel quite like sharing that with a guy that she'd decided she detested on sight.

'And Rowan?'

So he'd picked up on that? He was so irritating.

'Rowan was—is—my best friend. Got engaged to Jonathan last year.'

'Can't have been easy for you.' She narrowed

her eyes at him, trying to work out what his angle was. Because that sounded suspiciously like empathy, and she knew he wasn't down here empathising with her out of the goodness of his heart. He had to have an angle.

'We're all used to it. It's fine.' She finished her wine and headed to the fridge for the bottle. 'Want anything?' she asked, thinking that it wasn't giving too much away to do the absolute minimum of hostessing.

'A beer, if you have one.'

She snorted. Did he think she'd been born with a glass of Sauv in her hand? 'Yes, we have beer.'

She took the cap off a bottle and handed it over to him. 'So do you people eat?' he said, and if it had been said with any less hostility she might have confused his insult for the suggestion that they have dinner together.

She shrugged, tracing patterns in the condensation on her glass. 'I was waiting for Rowan to re-emerge.'

'So you all work and live and eat together. Nothing weirdly co-dependent about that at all...'

She rolled her eyes. 'It's temporary. Jonathan explained this, right? That we don't normally all live together like this. It's not exactly what any of us would choose.'

'God. It's bad enough that people get to own places like this. Then you whine about it?'

Liv raised her eyebrows, her glass raised halfway to her mouth,

'Judgemental much?' she asked, slightly surprised by his hostility. 'That's my family you're talking about. Just because I bitch about them doesn't mean you're allowed to.'

Adam took a stool across the breakfast bar from her and took a sip of his beer before answering. 'I'm just telling it how I see it. As far as I'm concerned it's immoral for one family to have so much wealth. Even if you do all live here together.'

Liv narrowed her eyes at him, not sure whether she was more impressed or annoyed with his bald honesty. 'Well, I apologise on behalf of late-stage capitalism,' she said. 'But you do know that I couldn't actually do anything about my family's accumulated wealth until I actually inherited it, and now I appear to be using it to house my entire family and whatever waifs and strays that they happen to encounter in the office.'

'Oh, right, this is a veritable homeless shelter,' he said with a humourless laugh. 'You're certainly doing everything you can for the poor.'

She stared at him a moment.

'Did anyone ever tell you you're a very rude house guest?'

'Yes, actually.' He leaned back against the countertop with his hands in his pockets and she momentarily didn't know whether to scratch his eyes out or drag her nails down his back. 'I get that a lot from the beneficiaries of inherited wealth.'

Her laugh took her so much by surprise that she snorted her wine.

'Why, Adam, anyone would think that you're trying to offend me.'

He smiled at that and it couldn't have been more different from the smirks that he'd sent in her direction earlier. His real smile was smaller, warmer. A twitch of the corner of his mouth, a crinkle at the corner of his eyes and a warmth that somehow projected from somewhere between the two. For a second, she forgot that that smile was entirely at her expense, and just enjoyed soaking it in. Until she remembered that he hated her and her family and apparently everything that they'd worked for over the decades. She shut down her face and made sure she wasn't smiling back. Because she still hated him and resented the fact that she was being forced to share her kitchen with him.

'Anyway, to answer your question, yes, we eat. I think there are leftovers in the fridge. But feel free to order takeout and eat in your room if it offends your sensibilities.'

'Me and Jonathan have work to do,' he replied. 'Might as well make it a working dinner.'

Liv fixed him with a stare. 'If it's regarding the fragrance project, then you need to be talking to me,' she reminded him, because she had no intention of being pushed out of her own project. But Adam shook his head, looking slightly indulgently at her in a way that made her certain she would go for the eyes first.

'Look,' he said, tilting his head as he spoke. 'I know you enjoy having this pet project, but if you're going to meet your ludicrously optimistic launch date, you really need me to take the lead on this. I'm sure you've been allowed a lot of leeway, but it's time to take this seriously.'

She folded her arms and glared at him. 'You think I'm not taking this seriously? Of course, because I'm a spoiled little princess who has feelings about things but can't actually do the work?'

Adam leaned back a little, regarding her carefully. 'Now you're just putting words—sexist words—in my mouth,' he argued. 'I'm just saying that the documentation I've seen so far speaks for itself.'

She strode over to him—well, a stride for her was probably a teeny-tiny fairy step for him, and she realised how close she had already been when she found herself having to tip her head back to look him in the eye. 'And I'm telling you,' she said, 'that if you want to see the documentation for *my* project, you should have come to the person working on the project full time—me—not the nearest available man.'

He shook his head, looking right down his nose at her. 'Oh, my God, would you stop making this about the fact that you're a woman?'

'You literally called me Princess,' she all

but hissed. 'You get that that makes you a textbook misogynist, don't you?'

'No,' he said slowly, drawing out the syllable, and she guessed that meant he thought he was about to get a good shot in. 'It means I hate spoiled little rich kids.'

She raised her eyebrows at him, arms still crossed over her chest. 'Glad we've cleared this up. Funny, though, how you don't seem to have a problem with Jonathan.'

'He comes with a reputation for how hard he works.'

That earned him a raise of her eyebrows. 'Ah, so you're judging us by reputation. That always ends well for young women. What do people say about me?'

He paused, considering, and she was surprised that he was pulling his punches. 'What would I need to hear other than that you're a Kinley? It doesn't take a genius to work out how you got the job.'

'Great,' she said, nodding and going back to her bar stool, taking another sip of her wine. 'Good to know exactly what you think of me.' He actually looked a little shamefaced, which took her by surprise, as if he only realised how judgemental he was being as the words left his mouth. She hated that she had to make concessions to get her work recognised but, if Jonathan had hired him and the contracts were signed, she had no hope of getting rid of him. Better work in the system she was faced with than waste her time raging against the machine.

'So do you want to see my research or not?' she asked, refusing to rise to the provocation of his words.

He simply nodded, and she pulled up her files on her iPad and slid it over to him. She didn't bother with nerves as he looked them over. She knew her work was good, regardless of what the gossip mill in the industry said about how she got her job. She'd studied management and marketing at university. Had worked in-house for several management consultancies on product launches before setting up her own consultancy. Jonathan had asked her to come in-house at Kinley more than once, but she'd always resisted before now, for all the reasons that Adam was making so clear to her.

If the family business hadn't been in so much trouble, she might still have said no. She couldn't think of anything worse than working with her brother, constantly having to prove her worth to him professionally, as well as personally. The aching dread of being pushed away gnawing at her. That feeling had been a constant companion since their parents had left them all, proof that unconditional love didn't, in fact, exist, and that the presence in her life of the people she loved the most was not something that she could rely on.

When Jonathan had told her that Kinley was in financial trouble and desperately needed a new line of income, and they had come up with the idea of developing the fragrance that her great-grandmother had once intended to launch, she had finally agreed to give it a try. The plans had been scrapped eighty years ago, and under normal circumstances her risk-averse brother would never have taken a gamble on something new. But after they'd all agreed to work together to save the business, she'd thought that he'd finally trusted her to do this. But it turned out she was wrong.

Jonathan had taken his responsibilities as head of the business and head of the family seriously—too seriously—and had committed himself to wrapping her in cotton wool and generally treating her like a child. If she'd thought that being engaged to a woman exactly her age would make him treat her like a grown-up, she'd been sadly mistaken. And she couldn't even complain to Rowan about it as she once would have done. She and Rowan were still working out how they made their friendship work now that Rowan was dating not only Livia's brother but her boss as well.

For a moment, the loneliness hit her like a flood. Rowan hadn't left her, she reminded herself, as she'd had to do several times in the past months when the gnawing ache had spiralled to a panic. Her best friend didn't love her any less than she had before she'd decided she loved Jonathan too. But regardless of how she tried to reason with herself, she couldn't help feeling that her best friend had slipped a little further away, and she was a little closer to being completely alone.

Talking about Jonathan with Rowan had to be off-limits, if their friendship was to survive, but the distance that forced into their relationship sometimes felt like a chasm between them. Livia had nowhere to go with her complaints about her brother, with the underlying fear that one day he would simply not be there.

She forced the feeling away. She didn't wallow. She hadn't when her parents had moved half a planet away. When they had boarded a plane without a backward glance and left her and her brothers to fend for themselves, and to deal with the hefty tax bill that they'd been running from.

At first she had thought that Rowan marrying into her family would bring them closer, and yet the easy intimacy that they'd once had was just out of reach. For a moment she yearned for simpler days when they could spend the their time lazing through study sessions with regular breaks for cheap coffee and cheaper wine.

She shook her head, trying to throw off her melancholy, realising too late that Adam was still there, watching her carefully now.

'What's wrong?' he asked her, and she fought down a shiver, hating that he, of all people, had seen something that she kept hidden from everyone.

'Nothing. Why would it be?' she lied. She heard two sets of footsteps on the stairs down to the kitchen and allowed herself a long breath of relief. She didn't like how much Adam seemed to see.

Rowan was rosy-faced and disgustingly cheerful when she appeared at the bottom of the stairs a minute later. 'Everyone ready for dinner?' she asked, going to the fridge and pulling out a foil-covered dish. Liv grunted a reply, not wanting either Rowan's or Jonathan's attention right now, so she grabbed cutlery from the drawer and set five places at the table. She shouted up the stairs for Caleb to get himself down here, half hoping that he had his noise-cancelling headphones on so that she would have to go and find him. But the universe was not her friend today, and she heard heavy footfalls above her. She went through the motions until they were all seated. Making small talk about the food while Jonathan topped up their glasses, making his self-appointed position as patriarch clear.

Caleb shovelled down his food, getting his obligatory family time out of the way so he could get back to his laptop. She wondered if she should ask him more probing questions about what he was doing up there. He was no stranger to working long hours, but, from the look on his face, he didn't look as if he'd just been dragged away from an eight-hour coding session. Jonathan and Rowan were doing their communicating-without-words thing, Rowan breaking off occasionally to remember that there were other people at the table and to ask Liv about her day.

She was hit by another wave of loneliness—not for what Rowan and Jonathan had. She didn't want someone to fall in love with her, she couldn't see that leading to anywhere other than disappointment, abandonment and pain. But until a few months ago, Liv thought, she'd at least had a *person*. At least after a breakup, you got to be angry with your ex, but she couldn't be angry at Rowan—especially not when she saw how happy she was, and how much easier her life was when Jonathan was happy as well.

Liv suppressed the sigh she could feel brewing and looked up from her wine glass, only to be struck hard in the face by the heavy weight of Adam's gaze, fixed firmly on her. She creased her forehead. Frowned at him. *What?*

'You okay?' he mouthed back. She rolled

her eyes at him. She could do without his false concern. She just didn't have the energy to work out what he was up to. She took another sip of her wine and flicked her eyes back to Adam. Still watching her. Well, she wasn't going to let him psych her out. She stared back. If he wanted to make this a contest, then she'd give him one.

He quirked an eyebrow with what looked like amusement when he realised what she was doing. And then, without looking away, he forked a huge spoonful of pasta into his mouth. She refused to smile. She wouldn't look at his mouth, though she was sure from glimpses in her peripheral vision that there was a smudge of sauce on his lower lip that would make her warm if she were to look at it directly. She stared until her eyes were dry and stinging, her food had gone cold and her wine warm. Finally, with one of those micro smiles and a shake of his head, he looked away. It took every ounce of her self-control not to pump a fist in the air at her victory. Instead, she finally dug into her pasta, emitting what she knew was a glow of smug self-satisfaction. Fine. It was childish, she knew it was childish. But she so rarely felt like a success. Especially in this company, so she was going to take her petty little win and cherish it.

Adam was shaking his head again as she realised that Jonathan was trying to get her attention. 'I was asking Adam about market research and he said I should talk to you.'

'What?' she said, trying to catch up and remind herself that this was a working dinner, kicking herself for falling for Adam's mind games, no doubt to distract her. No need to tell Jonathan that she was incompetent—why would he when he could simply scramble her brains and let her embarrass herself?

'Right. Market research,' she prompted herself. 'I have the reports from the latest focus groups in my inbox. We could all go through them together?' She ground the words out because the last thing she wanted was to give up her tight hold on her project. There was a reason why Adam hadn't got the full picture from Jonathan. She didn't trust him not to be disappointed at her work and decide that the company was better off without her after all. So she'd got into the habit of not sharing with her brother until the last possible moment, delaying the inevitable anxiety. But doing that had no doubt contributed to him deciding that she was so incompetent that he had to hire Adam to do her job for her.

She talked both Adam and Jonathan through the results of the latest research into packaging and branding. She was holding her own, even under Jonathan's questions and Adam's no-doubt critical silences. But she was happy with the report and it had thrown up a few interesting ideas she would come back to later.

'Right, enough shop talk,' Rowan said after an hour and a half, wrapping an arm around Jonathan's shoulder, kissing him on the cheek and smiling at Liv. They all owed Rowan one for saving them from themselves.

Out of the corner of her eye, she saw Rowan whisper in Jonathan's ear and co- lour rise in his cheeks. She fought down the urge to spew on the table. 'I'm, erm, going out,' Livia said without thinking the words through. When she'd already established that she had no one to party with. Fine. She was a grown-up. She could sip a drink at a table for one for a couple of hours while her brother and her friend…ugh, she was not going to think about that.

Caleb had already disappeared back to his lair, leaving the four of them at the increasingly uncomfortable table. 'You should take Adam,' Jonathan said, eyes still on Rowan, as if that were a perfectly reasonable thing to say, rather than completely deranged.

'I'm… I…' She was so shocked that she couldn't think of something to say.

'Sounds great,' Adam said, and she turned her glare on him. What the hell?

But he rose from the table and grabbed a leather jacket from where he'd thrown it over the back of a chair. Liv looked beseechingly at Rowan, but she clearly had other things on her mind. So she cleared their plates from the table and grabbed her bag. Was she seriously doing this? She just had to get out of the house and then she could ditch him. No way was she spending the evening with him.

He'd already invaded her work life and her home life. He didn't get to crash her social life too. She snorted to herself as she tucked her phone into her back pocket. *What* social life? She knew that drinking alone didn't count—she really shouldn't let it count. Didn't want Adam to find out that she didn't even have someone to go for a drink with any more. But if playing along was the fastest way out of here, then she'd pretend to go for a drink with Adam.

'Fine. Good. Let's go,' she said, getting away from Rowan and Jonathan before she saw something she couldn't unsee. She pulled on boots and a denim jacket at the front door and turned to see Adam watching her.

'What?'

'Nothing,' he said with a smirk that she wanted nothing more than to wipe off his face. She pulled the door open and shot him a frustrated look.

'Come on, then,' she said. 'Let's go.'

CHAPTER FOUR

SHE JOGGED DOWN the steps from the front door to the pavement, eyes fixed firmly ahead. She shoved her hands in her pockets and didn't look back to see if Adam was following. With any luck he'd walk the other way and leave her to her bottle of wine for one. But she heard his irritatingly long strides behind her until he was walking alongside and showing no sign of leaving her to be lonely in peace.

They walked in silence to the corner and she realised she had no idea where she was going. Her great-grandparents' choice of where to buy the town house that had been passed down through the generations didn't exactly chime with her idea of a good time. There was a champagne and toffs wine bar on the corner. Not her kind of place at all. A single glass would probably cost her a week's salary. But the most important thing was that it looked like the last place on earth that Adam would follow, so she pushed open the glass door. She'd order a tap water if she had to.

When Adam followed her inside, she didn't bother hiding her groan.

'Worried I'm going to embarrass you in front of your friends?' Adam asked with an expression that told her that he'd like nothing more than to make her uncomfortable. But the second he'd spoken she'd realised the problem. He was expecting her to be meeting people here. He'd tagged along to mess with her and now he was going to see the truth. That she'd left the only people in her life back at the house because she couldn't bear to be around them.

'So? Where are they?' he asked as she hesitated and glanced around the room, wondering what the odds were of there being a friend or a colleague or even a vague acquaintance. But she didn't recognise anyone.

As silent seconds ticked by, she felt him come to realisation by degrees. She waited for the gloating that she was sure had to come. But as she stared him down, braced for his barbs, she saw his face soften.

'Should we get a table?' he asked, and she was taken aback by his words and the soft look in his eyes and the kindness in his voice. She let herself be led to a table in a way that she would never have allowed if he hadn't been so weirdly...nice?

'So,' he said, once they'd taken a seat and ordered drinks. 'You didn't really have plans?'

'Wow, they did hire you for your huge analytical brain after all,' she said, her voice drier than the wine she'd ordered.

He ignored her deliberate taunt. 'Why lie?'

She shrugged. 'I wanted to get out of there.'

'Why not call a friend?'

She shifted in her seat, embarrassed. She hadn't realised until too late that she'd spent so much time at work that she'd lost pretty much all her friends but Rowan. There was that...*kind* look again, the one that she couldn't stand. She shrugged, covering.

'Last-minute decision. And I don't mind my own company.'

He nodded understandingly, which made her want to strangle him. 'Those are both very valid positions to take. But they don't explain the look on your face when we got in here. Why did you freeze?'

She thought for a moment. Wondering which reply would get him off this line of questioning. 'Just surprised that you followed me. I was wondering how I was going to get rid of you.'

That snort again.

'If that were true, we wouldn't be sitting here right now.'

She didn't have anything to say to that. 'You don't have plans either?' she asked, diverting attention from herself.

'I've been in Scotland for a few years. My speed dial down here isn't what it used to be.'

She had a sip of her drink, because she wasn't really sure what to make of that.

'I still don't get why you're here with me.' Dammit, she hadn't meant for that to come out sounding so…truthful. But now she was really curious. Why was he here, if not to mess with her?

'Why wouldn't I want to spend time with you?' he asked.

It was her turn to snort. 'Seriously? Like

we haven't been arguing every second since we met?'

'Not every second,' he said, with a look so heated that it didn't take a genius to work out what he'd been thinking about the moments that they weren't actively sniping at one another. She was worried—deeply worried—if he'd thought anything remotely along the lines of when she'd first met him, and had been far more interested in his forearms than the fact that he was completely irritating.

There was nothing wrong with a little one-sided fantasy, she knew. He never had to know the things that she'd imagined in her weaker, lonelier moments. But fantasies that ran both ways... Fantasies that might spill into real life... Absolutely not—far too dangerous. Even if she didn't detest this man. Even if he weren't effectively stealing her job from under her, she wouldn't get involved. He was just too...under her skin. Already. On day one. And she didn't like that sensation. Didn't like anyone closer than a comfortable arm's length away. If you let people closer than that, it hurt when they left. You could feel the space where they'd been. She'd healed around too many empty spaces already. She was so riddled with hollows that sometimes she didn't feel quite real, any more.

'Not every second,' she agreed with Adam, because apparently her brain resembled Swiss cheese too.

'So, is this your local?' Adam asked, glancing around the bar as if a member of staff might emerge from one of the booths and force him to drink something other than a beer. 'It's really not,' she told him. 'It was just the closest.'

He smiled. One of those tiny, secret, genuine ones that did bad things to her. 'You were that desperate to get rid of me?'

She groaned.

'Has anyone told you how irritating you are?'

'People generally find me quite charming.'

She full on belly-laughed at that, snorting wine through her nose and having to hold her sides until she could breathe normally again. She took a few shuddering inhales to make sure she had herself under control, and took the cocktail napkin that

Adam held out to her. She wiped her eyes and, mortifyingly, her nose, and when she looked up at Adam, something had shifted. She couldn't detest him as she had an hour ago, and the knowledge made her nervous. But there wasn't really anything she could do. That was the other thing. People were like barbed arrows. Once they got you, you couldn't get them out easily.

'I can't believe the idea of me being charming is so hilarious.'

'I can't believe that you think that you're charming. You must know that you're not. You've been glowering at me all day.'

'I don't want to be all "Yes, but…"'

'Yes, but?'

'You started yelling approximately three seconds after we met.'

'Because you were trying to steal my job!'

'I turned up for a meeting and accepted a consulting position without even knowing you were on the project. I don't think your fight is with me, babe.' She was so taken aback by that 'babe' that she didn't manage to put words in order and get them out of her mouth before he started to speak again. 'Your fight is with Jonathan—though I'm not sure I can blame him if you weren't sharing your work with him. But you can't have it out with Jonathan because he's marrying your best friend so you're taking it out on an innocent bystander. Me.'

She narrowed her eyes, hating how many hits he'd got in there. 'It's so impossible that I just disliked you on sight?' she asked, feigning innocence.

He took a sip of his beer, and she tried not to watch. Honestly tried. But his long, thick fingers wrapped around his glass caught her eye. And when she forced herself to look away from that, there was his throat, long, tanned, his Adam's apple moving as he drank. He put down the glass and she tried not to let her little lust diversion show.

'Come on. We can quit pretending. I don't think either of us is stupid enough to act on the fact that we're attracted to one another,' he said, as if he were commenting on nothing more controversial than the drinks menu. 'We might as well acknowledge it,' he went on. 'Clear the air. We'll get a lot more work done if we're not constantly at each other's throats because that's easier than admitting that we want each other.'

She stared at him for half a second, weighing up how much it would cost her to just agree with him. 'Oh, my God, your ego really knows no bounds, does it?' she said, refusing to let her voice waver.

He shrugged, leaning back in his seat and drinking. 'So which part isn't true?' he asked as he set his beer back on the table.

'The part where I'm attracted to you, for a start,' Liv said, her voice just a touch sharper than she wanted it to be. Adam smirked, and stretched an arm across the back of the booth. It pulled his T-shirt tight across pecs that belonged on a men's magazine cover, and pulled the fabric up to reveal a trail of hair under the waistband of his jeans. When she finally tore her gaze away and looked at his face, she realised he'd done it on purpose.

'I hate you,' she told him.

'So you've been thinking about me,' he said, looking as if he was deep in thought. 'And you say that you're not interested.'

The scale of his ego was enough to snap her out of the dark spell that Adam had somehow cast over her by stretching in a tight T-shirt.

'Fine. So what if I'd probably bang this out of my system if you had an entirely different personality?' Liv declared. 'Like you said: we're both too smart for that—and your personality is completely objectionable and I'm not a masochist.'

'So we just ignore it?' Adam nodded, leaning forwards and resting his elbows on the table. 'How would you feel about calling a truce?' he asked.

Liv frowned, trying to see if there was anything in his expression to tell her if he was being disingenuous. 'That definitely sounds like a trap,' she said carefully. 'I agree to a truce and all of a sudden your name is on my research reports, and my project, that I've been responsible for from day one, disappears from under my nose? No way. I'm not… I'm not going to start any trouble. But I'm not going to agree to not fight for something that's so important to me.'

'I wasn't planning on starting a fight,' Adam said.

Liv shook her head. 'Of course you're not. But you're planning on doing your job. And when what I think is right for the project comes into conflict with what you think is right, you're not going to try and pull rank and insist we do things your way? Because you know that's throwing the first punch.'

'I'm not in the habit of punching people at work. Believe it or not, I have other conflict resolution techniques up my sleeve. I'm a professional. Not just some bloke your brother pulled in off the street.'

'Fine, then. It's a truce, unless you throw a punch at my work.'

He finished the last of his beer and Liv glanced at the door. Would it be safe back at the house yet? If she and Adam had reached an uneasy truce, she didn't want to push that peace too far by dragging this evening out. She couldn't help but feel that staying for more than a single drink with Adam would end in a fight or, worse, some light groping.

'Shall we go somewhere else?' Adam asked, and she examined his face for ulterior motives. But, she told herself, talking about the fact that they were attracted to one another had robbed some of the power out of it. Now that he'd asked, it all seemed a little less dangerous. So she followed him out of the bar and they walked along shoulder to shoulder. Well, more like shoulder to elbow, given that he towered over her more than a foot.

They walked until they found a pub, noise and smokers spilling out onto the pavement. They went inside and it couldn't have been more different from their first venue. The building had to be hundreds of years old, and the walls and bar were panelled in rich, burnished oak. The real ale pumps were highly polished brass, and she ordered a pint of ale, because it would be wrong to drink anything else in these surroundings.

A real fire burned in the fireplace against the early-autumn chill, and beside it was the only free table, small and circular with two stools tucked underneath.

Livia ducked through the crowds to get the seats while Adam followed in her wake, carrying the drinks. The tiny space pressed them together with an intimacy that hadn't been there at the last bar. The warm buzz of chatter created a comfortable background noise, taking the pressure off the need to force conversation, and the minutes passed as quickly as the beer slipped down.

With the serious conversation out of the way, there was room for something more friendly. Smaller things, movies that they'd liked and comfort food they turned to and, when that started their stomachs rumbling, the bar snack and flavour of crisps they preferred when they were in a proper pub, rather than somewhere with wasabi nuts served in a miniature tea chest. They picked through a packet of cheese and onion, and then prawn cocktail, neither of them commenting on how those particular choices of flavour would help with their stated determination to not kiss each other.

They were eventually hustled out of the door half an hour after closing time with questions about whether they had homes to go to. She shivered when she walked outside—she'd been sitting by the fire for so long that her denim jacket didn't quite cut it. Adam shrugged out of his jacket and she watched him, confused, until he tried to drape it over her shoulders and she skipped out of his reach.

'What the hell are you doing?' she asked, with a tone of barely suppressed mortification.

'You looked cold,' Adam said, frowning and plainly confused.

Liv snorted. 'Of course I'm cold, I should have worn another layer. But how does you freezing to death because you're wearing nothing but a muscle tee help?'

Adam stopped dead on the pavement, hands on his hips as he looked down at her. 'This is a normal T-shirt,' he said, while his pose pulled it skintight across his shoulders, arms and chest, which rather proved her point.

'Then how come I can count your abs?' she asked, attempting an air of innocence, but ruining the effect entirely by licking her lips.

'Maybe because you can't help looking,' Adam asked.

Her breathing faltered, because he was right and she absolutely hated that. Almost as much as she hated that he'd noticed. He was a looming presence in front of her, the lamp post behind him casting him in shadow. Maybe it should have intimidated her. She shivered again, and it was nothing to do with fear, or the cold.

It was all to do with him. The fact that she had been looking at his muscled torso all night, even though she'd tried not to. The deep charcoal of the fabric creasing into perfectly symmetrical contours. Six, no, eight well-defined ridges below his broad chest.

'So, you don't want my jacket,' Adam said, thoughtfully. 'And I don't want you to be cold. Any ideas how we can warm you up?'

She was so panicked at the million different ways that she wanted to answer that question but knew that she couldn't if she wanted to retain any sense of sanity. Finally the words that left her mouth, quite without her meaning them to, were, 'Race you!'

You would think that being best friends with an ultrarunner, that acting as support crew for someone who frequently ran a hundred miles *for fun*, she might have picked up a few tips. Like, not marathon-running skills, but perhaps the ability to reach the end of the street without feeling like she might die. Unfortunately, it turned out that cardio health wasn't something you absorbed by osmosis, and she had to lean over at the end of the street, resting her hands on her knees, trying to catch her breath.

Adam strolled up with that long easy stride,

not an eyebrow out of place, while she was there with her hands on her knees, gasping for breath, wondering whether she'd left a lung in the gutter somewhere. 'Hot,' Adam commented as he reached her while she was still struggling for air. 'Really hot.'

'Stop making fun of me while I'm dying,' she managed to gasp.

Adam only crossed his arms and leaned against the lamp post. 'Stop making it look so funny, then. How did you get to be such a gifted athlete? Please, tell me your secret.'

'Stop it,' she said again. 'Rowan does my share of physical exercise. I carry her sandwiches.'

He laughed again, the utter pig. 'Well, then, I'm glad I didn't try and beat you. I would have embarrassed myself.'

She stood up straight and narrowed her eyes at him. She took a step forward, somehow forgetting that that would only bring her eyeline to his nipples, rather than his face. And she didn't exactly feel the boost of confidence she'd hoped to get from being eye to eye. Especially as she didn't even seem to be able to lift her eyes to meet his for several long seconds. She'd never minded being short before. Other than her brothers teasing her when they were kids.

Her best friend was nearly a whole foot taller than her. But this, standing with her chin by Adam's chest, the sheer size of him unavoidable, was the absolute tiniest and most helpless she had ever felt. She tipped her chin up, thinking that somehow that would help, but she realised immediately that she'd made a gross miscalculation, because this was far more intimate than she'd been prepared for. And that was before Adam's hands came to each side of her face. His palms skimmed her cheeks, his thumbs skittering along the ridges of her cheekbones. They stopped just in front of her ears, the tips of his fingers hitting every sensitive spot along her hairline before pressing just hard enough to the nape of her neck to force a half-gasp, half-groan from her lips.

'How's the breathing going?' he asked with a self-satisfied smirk that suggested that he'd forgotten the very sensible conversation they'd had earlier about acknowledging their attraction taking the power out of it.

'Uh huh,' she breathed, knowing that it

didn't answer his question at all. Aware too late that it gave away far too much about how she felt about him.

He laughed at her, gently. But it wasn't unkind. Didn't make her bristle the way so many of his comments had. Instead it made her melt and she had to look down and make sure she wasn't a puddle at his feet.

But she'd somehow forgotten his hands on either side of her face. He turned her face back up to look at him, and she could see the indecision in his eyes. That he wanted this—her—but wouldn't let himself take it. And somehow his reluctance set off a self-preservation instinct that her own doubts hadn't. She took a step back and he dropped his hands but didn't take his eyes off her.

'Talking about it was meant to stop stuff like this happening,' she observed, and Adam nodded but didn't look away.

'Feels like *stuff like this* is going to be hard to ignore.'

'We should probably be more careful,' Livia said. But she didn't move, and neither did he, and they were just standing there under a lamp post on the corner of a London street, waiting for something to rescue them from their own worst impulses. It was a police van that did it in the end, blazing past with sirens and flashing lights and so close to the kerb that she took a step backwards to be sure she wasn't in its path.

They continued to stare at each other in the fading red and blue flashes, and then turned, in sync, to walk back towards the house.

'So, any bright ideas how we stop something like that happening again?' she asked.

'You could stop literally running away from situations that make you uncomfortable,' Adam suggested.

'You were the one being suggestive. Running away was supposed to help.'

He snorted. 'Please, for God's sake, don't *help* by doing anything else that will require mouth-to-mouth resuscitation. And no more drinking together. It was a stupid idea to even come out like this. Tomorrow I'm going to give you the cold shoulder and you're going to thank me for it.'

Liv nodded.

She should really hate him talking to her like that. She hated being told what to do. So she absolutely shouldn't be feeling her nipples go hard at the thought of it. It was a cold night, she told herself. That was a much more reasonable explanation for her reaction than Adam going all alpha on her.

'It'll be like you don't even exist,' she promised him.

CHAPTER FIVE

HE DIDN'T EVEN exist for Liv—and that was exactly as it should be, Adam thought as he got ready for work. He'd barely caught sight of her for a week, and at last the tight-chested feeling he got when he thought about that moment on the street when they'd so nearly done something stupid had started to loosen. They'd been idiots, straying far too close to things that would have messed up his job and his life and—well, everything, really.

He'd never been particularly interested in a relationship before, but he'd never been terrorised by the thought of one either, not the way that Livia terrified him. She moved so…easily through the world. Tripping up the front steps of the grand regency house as if that was just what people did. As if it were a perfectly ordinary place for someone to live. She didn't stop in front of the grand facade and gaze up at it, which he was sure must be a normal reaction to such polished grandeur. Her obliviousness to it felt like fingernails across freshly grazed skin. Raw and sharp. He resisted hissing out a breath at another of those waves of resentment he'd felt ever since he'd met this family.

The house was big enough that they'd managed to stay out of each other's way for days, but even so he should probably never have agreed to stay here. He should have known how such blatant unearned privilege would grate on him. But old habits died hard. He could have booked a different hotel—the cost had already been budgeted and accounted for, after all—but Jonathan had offered him a place to stay free of charge and the compulsion to save whenever he could was as ingrained in him as his name.

Would he have made the same decision if he'd known it would cost him his peace of mind? He laughed, grimly, to himself. Probably. Some things were worth more than peace of mind. Things like a roof over his head and breakfast in the morning. Three meals a day, every day. But it wasn't the offer of a spare room or the streets, he reminded his rapidly beating heart.

It didn't matter how many times he told himself that things were different now. His body had learned its fears and responses when he was still in primary school. It wasn't just going to unlearn them now. He didn't want to unlearn it anyway. Never knew when you might need those instincts again. No one planned on becoming homeless. He knew his mother hadn't. She had worked every hour in the day to pay the rent on their flat and put food on the table morning and night. Extra hours in the school holidays when he didn't get free school lunches and there were babysitters to pay for. It had been a finely balanced system that had worked…until it hadn't.

A fender bender in a supermarket car park had made her car undrivable, which had meant that she hadn't been able to reach half of her cleaning jobs. Their income had only been just enough to pay the rent and they'd fallen short first one month then another. He hadn't been supposed to know any of this, of course. But he'd overheard his mum on the phone. Seen the way she looked at the letters that landed on the doormat almost every morning.

And there had been no missing packing a single holdall of his things and staying on a procession of sofas. Occasionally, if they were lucky, a spare room for a while. When he'd reached his teens, he'd started working part-time but his mother wouldn't let him drop out of school. The day after he sat his final A-level exam he started a job in the city. Had talked his way onto a training scheme that usually only took graduates. Had saved every penny until he'd had a deposit and first month's rent on a flat. And then every penny after that until they could afford one with a second bedroom— he'd insisted his mum take the one bedroom in their first place. Another six months of sleeping on a sofa bed wasn't going to do him any harm.

The first night he'd had his own bedroom since his age had been in single figures, he'd shut the door and let the relief wash over him in waves. It was only the next day when it was all still there—the panic, the fear, the checking and rechecking the door, the post, their bank balance—that he'd realised having a door to close wouldn't be enough to keep all those away. That he'd realised for the first time that he'd thought that those were things that could be left behind, rather than something that was so much a part of him that it was baked into his bones.

Most of the time it was just there, quiet, under the surface. Buried so deep inside that he didn't even notice it any more. And then he'd see something, smell something, bump into someone he went to school with, and he was a child again, waiting for a long, hungry afternoon to pass.

And sometimes he'd dream. When he'd slept last night, he'd been back in the damp-smelling room they'd lived in for a few months round the corner from Livia's house. He could still feel the moisture in the walls under his fingertips, the peeling paint on the flimsy door to their single room. The broken lock on the shared bathroom door.

He'd woken from the dream with a start, stumbled, still not really awake, towards the bathroom he shared with Liv, and when he'd flicked the light switch, he'd been paralysed with confusion, staring at the marble basins and gold taps where he'd been expecting paint-flecked avocado and chipped Formica.

And then he'd caught some sort of movement across the room and realised two things at once: one, he had frozen in the doorway to the bathroom—the shared bathroom. And two, he'd been wearing only his boxers. He'd looked up as the second door to the bathroom had opened, revealing Livia in the doorway, wearing little more than he was. She'd clutched her robe a little tighter around her when she'd realised she wasn't alone.

'Adam! What the…?'

He'd opened his mouth to speak but realised he didn't know how to explain this.

How opening the bathroom door had unleashed waves of memories and anger and half-forgotten resentments. And how much, right then, that had all been turned on her and her family. Instead, all he'd been able to do was scowl at her, slam the door, and stop himself saying something that would have made a bad situation even worse.

Some damage had already been done— that was undeniable, even though Livia hadn't said a word since he'd slammed the door in her face. But he'd heard it in the way that she'd been crashing around in the cabinets. The aggressive slam of the door on her side of the room, an angry bookend to his own.

Oh, he knew that the Kinleys had had their share of tribulations. Who hadn't read about their parents' attempts to not pay the taxes that, in theory, stopped the least well off from starving in the streets? But they'd had grandparents who'd inherited a property portfolio from *their* parents, and who in turn left it to the Kinley siblings, meaning that they could raise the capital needed to appease the authorities, and still have this house and a couple of others left over.

They could cry all they wanted about how badly that had affected them, but they didn't have a clue about how hard life could really be.

How hard some people worked just to keep a roof over their heads, never mind to live in this sort of luxury.

He'd barely got back to sleep before his alarm had woken him at five. His steps were reluctant as he went down to the kitchen, hoping for a cup of coffee to kickstart his brain before he made his way into the office. Perhaps if Jonathan was already up he could give him a lift. He and Liv had managed not to see each other before work all week and he didn't want to break that run now. But to his annoyance, taking him off-guard again, it was Liv who was sitting at the kitchen island, coffee in hand as she swiped through something on her iPad.

She greeted him with a scowl.

He tapped on his phone while he was eating and pulled up an app to order a car. 'Don't bother,' Livia said, glancing up and seeing what he was doing. 'I'll drive, but I'm leaving in five minutes so you'd better get a move on.'

A monosyllabic communication style had held strong for a week now so he just said, 'Fine,' and avoided eye contact. They had been different people that night in the pub. Somehow he'd managed to ignore that she came from everything that he hated. He'd fallen victim to his libido, had seen everything that he liked about her and had somehow managed to ignore everything that he hated. Until he'd dreamed about his old life and found himself so out of place in her home that he had frozen solid.

He'd been distracted by a pretty face, he

realised. Distracted from everything that was important to him. His values. The ones that his mother had instilled in him. He tried to imagine what his mother would make of her—a woman whose job and home and whole secure, prosperous future had been handed to her at birth.

Why was he even thinking like that? His mother was never going to meet Livia. He would be working with her for six months and then he'd never see her again. But he'd been irritated by colleagues before, and had never found himself worrying about what his mother would think about them. And many of them had been richer and stupider and more privileged than Livia. But he'd never cradled any of their faces between his hands either.

The conflict he felt between how utterly right it had felt to have her standing in front of him, below him, looking up at him with her lip between her teeth and so clearly holding herself back, waiting to see if he would make the first move. It had been a gift to her, that control, as if she knew exactly how much he liked having her at his mercy. There was a reason he hadn't let himself think about it. It would be utterly dangerous for her to know how perfect she felt for him, sometimes.

'I'm leaving—are you ready?' she said, and he looked up. The expression on real Liv's face so different from the tightly wound lust that he'd seen there the night they'd gone to the pub.

Liv parked the car in a reserved space outside the great steel and glass facade of Kinley Head Office.

Her great-grandparents' had bought this building in the nineteen twenties, and it had somehow survived the financial cuts that had been made to pay the tax bill her parents had run from. Apparently they could generate more income by leasing out some floors than by selling the whole thing outright.

Sometimes she wished that they'd just got rid of it. Another link to her family gone. She didn't need a building to remind her of how her parents had cut her out of their lives. She had been able to understand, sort of, that they had had to leave when the money had run out and everything had hit the fan. She could have understood anyone doing that. But it didn't explain why they had left her behind.

It was okay because she was eighteen, they'd said. In her first year at university. There was no need to turn her life upside down to leave the country with them. Especially as Jonathan was there to keep an eye on her in the holidays. It would be difficult to keep in contact regularly at the start—she'd expected that while they found somewhere to stay and got settled. But as months and then years had passed with barely more than an email a few times a year, she'd had to draw the conclusion that they simply didn't care enough to make the effort to see her. They had abandoned her. Left her behind and not looked back, even for a second.

That was part of why she had resisted Jonathan's attempt to give her a job. Because being here always reminded her of her parents, and she really had no desire to be constantly thinking about the people who were meant to love her unconditionally but had been able to walk away from her with barely a backward glance.

But something about dragging Kinley into the twenty-first century while harking back to its heritage appealed to her. She'd been working in marketing luxury goods—she'd never intentionally leveraged it, but her surname was Kinley, and her brother was the CEO of one of the oldest British luxury brands. She wasn't naive enough not to believe that had opened doors. She'd made a point of working harder than was always called for, to stave off accusations of nepotism—for her own ego as much as anything. And she liked to think that she'd earned a reputation for hard work and impactful campaigns. But apparently that reputation hadn't reached Adam, who had made no secret about turning his nose up at her being given this job by her big brother.

'About last night,' Adam said, just when she'd started to wonder whether they were going to make this awkward silence permanent.

She raised her eyebrows, waiting for him to continue.

'I wasn't staring at you.'

She frowned.

'It felt quite a lot like staring, when you were just standing there looking at me,' she said, glancing at him from the corner of her eye as she slid from the car and locked it behind her.

'I wasn't, I promise,' Adam said. He walked around to her side of the car and fixed her with a serious look that stopped her, made her look up at him, remember how much she'd liked the way he had loomed over her when they'd walked home from the pub the week before.

'Then what were you doing?' she asked, wishing that she'd managed to make her voice a little steadier. But she still had the upper hand, she promised herself, because she couldn't see a way for him to talk himself out of this one, however silver-tongued he could be when he tried.

'I was thinking.'

'About my bathroom?' Liv asked.

'Sort of, I suppose,' Adam said with a shrug that looked slightly stiff. 'About your house, in general. I kind of zoned out, and I know I should have turned away as soon as I realised that you were there and I'm sorry that I didn't. That was inappropriate of me.'

Liv narrowed her eyes. 'We're colleagues who share a bathroom. I think we passed inappropriate a while ago.'

'It won't happen again. That's all I'm trying to say.'

'Why did my bathroom make you zone out?' Liv asked, knowing that she was missing something vital, and for some reason finding that irritating. It shouldn't, she knew. It shouldn't bother her that she couldn't figure this man out. He shouldn't be anything to her, but she couldn't shake his expression when he'd stood in the doorway of her bathroom, and she wanted to know what had put that look on his face.

His lips disappeared in a thin, flat line, and she knew that he was holding back. For some reason that irked her. 'No, tell me,' she prompted him. 'I really want to know.'

'It's just so…over the top,' he told her, shaking his head.

She laughed. 'I know, it's not exactly my taste either…' but her voice died off when she saw the expression on his face. 'This isn't about my great-grandmother's taste in interior design, is it?'

He had no reason to tell her this stuff. Had no idea why all these ghosts of feelings he'd thought that he'd long dealt with were coming up now. Perhaps it was being back in London after so long. Seeing first-hand the sort of lives that were being lived literally around the corner from where he and his mother had eked out a living while sleeping on other people's sofas. He found himself completely unable to hide that from Liv. She'd seen him half naked, all his fears on show, and it was harder than he could have expected to pile those protective layers back on again.

'It's just very different from what I knew growing up. I still find it hard to believe sometimes that all this was just around the corner the whole time. Literally and metaphorically. The metaphorical part I've been getting to grips with over the years. The literal parts only started hitting me since I've been back. It's weird being somewhere so familiar and so alien at the same time.'

'You lived near here?'

He had to laugh. He couldn't have been further from this if he'd actively tired.

'For a while anyway. My mum and I stayed with a friend on Gosford Street.'

He saw her flinch and couldn't even blame her. He'd flinched when they'd walked up the street the first time, the high-rise apartment building looming at the end of the road.

'Did you stay there long?'

'A few months. Even good friends lose patience with you living on their sofa eventually.'

There was no way that she could understand what it would have been like for him. And maybe that was the beauty of it. She would no more be able to grasp the precariousness of his childhood than if he'd explained the ocean to a pampered goldfish kept in a marble-lined kitchen.

'So you moved around a lot as a child?' she asked as they walked through the lobby of the Kinley building.

'Something like that, I guess.'

'You guess? I'm trying to make small talk here and you're being less forthcoming than your average murder suspect. I didn't realise the details of your life were going to be classified information.'

'Not classified. But not everyone's childhood lends itself to sharing. Your privilege is showing again, Princess. It's not much fun explaining to strangers that you basically didn't live anywhere in particular for large parts of your childhood.'

She stood staring at him and he could see the cogs turning as she processed what he had just said. Dammit. It wasn't as if his experiencing homelessness was a secret. Objectively he knew that it was nothing to be ashamed of. But he found it hard to talk about, which meant he did so rarely, which in turn meant that most people simply didn't know that it had happened. They had reached her office, which was where they should have parted ways and got on with their day, avoiding each other as much as possible. But he couldn't just walk away after saying something like that. So when she opened the door to her office he followed her in, standing in front of her as she propped her hip against her desk and crossed her arms, waiting for him to speak.

'You were homeless?' she asked, her voice wavering slightly, presumably because she knew that she was on fragile ground.

'I periodically experienced homelessness,' Adam corrected her. 'We didn't sleep in an underpass. But we didn't have a permanent home either,' he said on a sigh. For some reason, he knew that keeping the truth from her was only delaying the inevitable.

'We?' Liv asked, and he was pleased for the reprieve of her asking about the 'who' of the situation, rather than focussing on the fact that he'd had nowhere to live. He would always be happy to talk about his mum.

'My mum and me,' he said, and something of how he felt about her must have shown on his face because Liv smiled back at him.

'You two are close?' she asked, and he saw something yearning in her expression. He softened his voice, remembering what he knew about the Kinley parents, and how they'd fled the country on the back of their tax scandal.

'Yeah,' Adam said. 'We both lived in London until she got married a few years ago and moved up to Scotland, and I decided to go too. I travelled a bit after that. It felt strange being here without her.'

'And your dad?'

Adam shrugged, because there wasn't anything to tell there. 'He's never been on the scene. Never missed him.'

'Well, there's something we have in common. Terrible dads.' Liv's wry smile didn't hide the obvious hurt in her voice when she spoke about that. 'I'm not sure that's something we should drink to,' she added, her voice slightly flat.

He let one corner of his lip turn up. 'I'm not sure we should be drinking to anything at seven-thirty in the morning.'

'Or together at all. I thought that was what we decided.'

Of course it was, because it was far too dangerous for them to have conversations that were anything other than strictly professional. They had come far too close to doing something stupid the week before, and they would have to take care not to find themselves in that sort of position again.

He had an idea for how to put some space between them. For a couple of days at least. He just needed Jonathan's buy-in before he told Liv.

'Can you meet me in my office in an hour?' he asked. 'There's something I need to talk to you about.'

Liv looked surprised, but agreed. 'Of course. I'll see you then.'

CHAPTER SIX

'So what's this about?' Liv asked, walking into Adam's office, her arms crossed across her chest to remind herself as much as him that she was to concentrate on maintaining distance between them. But she drew up short when she walked into the room and found Jonathan already there. Were they going to spring more surprises on her?

'So,' Adam said as she took a seat at the table, looking directly at Jonathan. 'I've been looking over all the emails and meeting notes with the parfumier and I don't think there's anything more that we can do without visiting in person. Liv's gone back and forth on the phone and by email and we're not any further—'

'I've been doing every—' Liv tried to cut in, but Adam just spoke over her.

'I don't doubt it,' he said. 'And you've

pushed him as far as I think you're able. I know you have a trip planned next month but I don't think it can wait that long. I want to go before the end of the week, which means we need all the briefing documents finished before I go.'

'Before *you* go?' Liv asked, trying to keep a lid on her temper. There was absolutely no way that he was going to take this from her. She'd put in too much work to turn this over to someone who had only been working with them for a little over a week.

'You've said yourself how busy you are, and we don't seem to be getting anywhere with this one. I thought a change of tack might help, and it would take something off your plate as well,' Adam tried to explain.

'Oh, no,' Liv said, her anger making her laugh. 'Getting Gaspard to agree to our schedule is the most crucial part of the project. This is my baby and I'm not going to let you—'

'Liv, stop,' Jonathan said, and she turned to glare at her brother. After all the effort he had put into their relationship since he had started seeing Rowan, and now he was going to take Adam's side…

'I agree with Liv,' Jonathan said, turning

to Adam, and her jaw dropped with disbelief. 'This was her idea, and she knows the background better than anyone. She already has the relationship with Gaspard. It doesn't make sense not to use that.'

'Jonathan.' Adam squared up to the other man, and she saw her brother note it and his hackles rise. 'I appreciate you wanting to defend your sister, but—'

Liv watched as Jonathan pinched the bridge of his nose and winced.

'I am not in the mood to referee this right now,' Jonathan said, his jaw tightly clenched. 'Both of you go to Paris, and if you could find a way to work together without giving me the stomach ulcer I'm so desperately trying to avoid I think we would all be grateful.'

With that last rebuke, Jonathan walked out of the office, leaving her alone with Adam.

'We can't both go. That's a terrible idea,' Liv said as soon as Jonathan was gone. The very last thing she needed in her life right now was a weekend in Paris with this man who she knew it was so important that she resist.

'I agree, but I want to be in on this, so the only solution is that we both go,' Adam said, mirroring her body language and giving her a challenging look. 'Like your brother said.'

Liv shook her head, because that was madness, and he had to know it. 'You know that's not a good idea, we said—we *both agreed*—that we need to be more careful around one another. We don't want to start something that can only end badly. A trip to Paris together is a terrible idea.'

He raised an eyebrow, not backing down. Then he took a step towards her, arms still crossed, a dangerous look on his face. 'You're going to find it that hard to resist me?'

'You think it's *my* self-control we need to worry about?' Liv asked, wishing her voice hadn't chosen that moment to wobble. Ugh, he was so, so right. When he looked at her like that it was all too easy to forget herself. 'You're not as pretty as you think you are,' she told him, doing her best not to show that she was affected by him at all. 'And Paris is just a city. If I can resist jumping your bones here, I'm not going to struggle just because we're the other side of the Channel.'

'Great. I'll get Maria to make the arrangements.'

She gave him a strong look. 'If we get there

and it turns out there's only one bed, you're sleeping in an alleyway, so don't even think about it.'

'We're never going to get through all of this tonight.' Liv groaned long after she would normally have headed out for dinner. Her assistant had managed to book last-minute flights, but she'd taken *as soon as possible* as literally as she could, which meant that they were flying out at seven the next morning, when she'd normally be having her breakfast, and that meant pulling an all-nighter to get the briefing documents ready to present the next day.

She had been collating market research for more than three hours in the quiet of her office, keeping herself blissfully distracted from the knowledge that first thing tomorrow morning she would be flying to the most romantic city in the world with a man whose body she desperately wanted. Probably enough to ignore his entirely objectionable personality if she didn't have her guard up at all times. But she had put together all of her own research and she'd taken these briefing documents as far as she could without consulting with Adam on his parts of it. She had been waiting for him to come to her, not wanting to show the weakness of needing him, even in a professional capacity. But they didn't have time to mess around playing games, so she pushed her chair back and walked confidently from her office, and rapped on Adam's door.

He looked up as she pushed open the door, and she saw the start of a smile on his lips before he caught himself and stopped it in its tracks.

'Everything going okay?' he asked, with his face and voice professionally neutral.

'I've finished with the research section. We need to put it together with your financials and go over the whole thing together.'

Adam nodded. Clearly he agreed that they had delayed being in the same room for as long as possible. It would be good practice for the two straight days they were about to spend in one another's company.

She sat in the chair the other side of the desk from Adam, at once hating the power dynamics it created but grateful for the solid piece of furniture between their bodies. An entirely immovable barrier between them if their self-control alone wasn't enough.

'This is good,' Adam said, looking through the pages that she had slammed onto the desk between them.

'No need to sound so surprised. Did you think I was here for my winning personality? Or did you simply think it was the Kinley name that got me through the door?'

'Are you denying that your name helped you?'

'What would you like me to do about it? I can't change who my parents are. God knows, if that had been an option I would have taken it a long time ago. Did you miss the part where they walked out and abandoned me?'

It was only as she took a couple of deep, slow breaths that she realised at some point she had got to her feet and raised her voice. Adam leaned back in his chair and held up his hands as a peace gesture.

'I'm sorry. I clearly hit a nerve.'

'Don't make out I'm being oversensitive. If you're going to imply that I'm somehow lucky in my parentage, you can deal with me being annoyed at you. This is cause and effect. Don't annoy me if you don't want me to be annoyed.'

'I just think that this would go easier if you accept your name has given you a leg-up in this business.'

'And *we* would get along a lot better if you would accept that the deeply traumatic effects of being abandoned by the parents who treated you as a princess for the first eighteen years of your life—while simultaneously dragging your family name into disgrace—might balance out some of that privilege. If you could just for a minute stop obsessing over the things I had that you didn't, you might be able to see that I've not had things as easy as you seem to think. That you have things that I'd gladly give up everything for.'

He let out a long breath, his eyes soft as he looked at her. 'Liv, I'm sorry, I didn't think.'

She shook her head, because no, he hadn't thought. 'You didn't think that spoilt rich kids have things tough sometimes too? That we can hurt? Maybe just occasionally you should count your blessings before you go on about how easy I've had it, and how tough it's been for you.'

She slumped back in her chair, feeling suddenly exhausted. She'd had no idea that emotional outpourings were so tiring. No wonder she didn't make them a regular event. No, she had to wait until she was stuck on a deadline in an office with a man she badly wanted to dislike and just as badly wanted to kiss. Because that was clearly the ideal time to lose your chill.

'You need a break,' Adam said, and she took his ignoring her outburst as a peace offering. It was a gift, really, not to have to think any more about the things that she had said.

'We both need one. And something to eat.' And with that he walked out of his office, pulling on his leather jacket and leaving her watching his behind as he headed for the bank of lifts.

Liv looked through his parts of the briefing documents while he was gone, dovetailing their work together and highlighting any areas that would need more work before they could say that they were done for the night. She glanced at her watch. They were going to be here until two, three o'clock at this rate. She wasn't even going to make it home to pack a suitcase. She sent off an urgent message to Rowan, asking her to throw a few things in a bag and send it over with Jonathan first thing in the morning. Her best friend shacking up with her brother had to have some advantages at least.

She looked up from Rowan's message telling her not to work too hard to the sound of the lift arriving back at their floor. Adam stepped out of the elevator enveloped by the smell of excellent Thai food from the place on the corner, and she honestly could have kissed him if they hadn't already agreed that that would be a very bad idea.

'I take everything back. You're my hero,' she told him, pushing their work to one side to make room for the food on his desk. Adam emptied out the carrier bags and lifted the lids on fragrant curries, fluffy white rice and a *pad thai* topped with toasted peanuts.

'We can't work with empty bellies,' Adam said, handing over bamboo cutlery and chopsticks.

Or fight, Liv silently added, because they hadn't exactly been working before he'd headed out. She talked through some of the gaps in their work that she'd found as they ate, which would have been a lot easier if she hadn't kept getting distracted by the way his fingers held his chopsticks. How her gaze was drawn to follow up to his lips. The amusement in his eyes when he caught her looking and his whole expression lit up.

'That was part one,' Adam said when the food was gone and the containers cleaned away.

'Part one of what? And of how many?' Liv asked, suspicion heavy in her voice.

'Of "we have a lot to do tonight and we're going to burn out if we don't take breaks".'

He stood up and came round to her side of the desk, holding out one hand to help her up and brandishing a set of keys in the other.

She hesitated for a moment. 'Where did you get those, where are you taking me and should I share my location with a friend?'

Adam tsked at her. 'Such little faith in me. I got chatting to the security guard. Turns out we went to the same school, I mentioned we needed a break and he let me in on a secret.'

She followed Adam up a flight of stairs, down a corridor where the floorboards were coated in a thick layer of dust, with just a few footprints on one side.

'I'm still getting quite strong serial-killer vibes, just so you know,' she told him.

'I am devastated that you have so little trust in me.' As he spoke, Adam searched through the keys until he found a long, old-fashioned type in heavy brass. The lock didn't seem to want to cooperate at first, but then gave way with a heavy clunk, and the doorway opened onto the sky.

Well, technically, it gave way onto a flat roof and a fire escape five stories up. But it was a flat roof and a fire escape with an unimpeded view all the way out across the city of London.

'This is incredible,' she breathed. 'From now on you're always in charge of making friends with the security guard.'

There was a mossy old set of patio furniture with a rather newer looking lighter and ashtray at the centre, which at least answered the question of what the security guard used this place for.

'Let's work out here for a bit,' Adam suggested, and Liv nodded her agreement. She'd lived in London her whole life and had been a part of the Kinley family just as long. But occasionally something came along—a new view of the world—which made her entirely re-evaluate what she thought she knew about it.

She needed to write, now, while she could feel the city pulsing around her. While she was at once in the heart of it and high above, able to see it as it truly was in a way that was lost at ground level. She could see the dark shell of Grenfell tower just a mile away, and Canary Wharf blinking at her in the distance. When she looked down there were headlights and phone lights and streetlights, and when she looked up she could just make out the stars.

Sitting atop the headquarters of the family business, she could feel the Kinley blood in her veins, feel all the ways that she was connected to this company, this brand, that went back more than a hundred years. And at the same time, she was something new. She was the incomer who was going to show this brand and this business what it could be again, if it were to take a risk some time.

'I don't know that look,' Adam said when he returned with their laptops, looking at her with an air of slight concern. 'Should I be worried?'

'This is my inspired face,' she said, opening her laptop, 'and you should only be concerned if you're intimidated by my brilliance.' He smirked and opened his own laptop, calling up the shared document they had both been working on.

'Would you stop deleting that paragraph?' Liv snapped half an hour later when he'd done it for the third time. 'I'm tired of pasting it back in.'

'Then take the hint and stop doing it,' Adam replied, not breaking the rhythm of his typing. 'We don't need it. You've made all the same points elsewhere.'

'But I make them best there.' She backspaced through a particularly verbose section on their ideal consumer that Adam kept trying to get past her.

'Kill your darlings, babe,' he said, in a sardonic tone that made her want to gouge his eyes out.

'But it's so much more fun killing yours.'

She looked up and made eye contact before very deliberately highlighting and hitting delete on the page he was working on.

He didn't back down from the challenge of her stare, but instead stood up, very slowly, planting his palms on the table and letting them take his weight. Was this meant to be threatening? Liv wondered, crossing her arms and looking him in the eye before he dipped his head and leaned in closer, closer, and—oh, my God, was he going to kiss her? Liv watched him move towards her, knowing that she should be putting a stop to this, but instead licking her lips, and wishing to God that she'd brushed her teeth after their Thai food.

If this was a test, she was going to fail it miserably, she thought as Adam continued to move so slowly towards her that her mouth was watering, her bottom lip caught between her teeth in anticipation, and then finally leaned all the way across the table and—

Shut. Her. Laptop.

'What the hell?' she asked, standing up so abruptly that her chair clattered to the floor behind her. Adam stood across the table from her, hands nonchalantly in his pockets, his expression unbearably smug. He shrugged.

'Seemed like I should stop you before you deleted everything we've written tonight.'

'Before *I* did?' she asked, realising that her voice sounded strangled as Adam closed his own laptop too, casually picked up his things and gestured towards the door that led back inside. 'I think I'm done here. Going to head back to my office.'

She was absolutely not letting him have the last word and walk away from her. 'Well, you might be done here, but I'm not,' she said, following him to the door. 'You were the one telling me to make cuts,' she pointed out.

'Yes—to the parts that you had written,' he said, striding down the corridor so that she had to keep doing little trotting half-steps to keep up. She was certain that he was doing it on purpose.

'You know that I hate you, don't you?' she asked, her voice deadly serious as they reached the stairs. 'The best part of launching this perfume isn't going to be that it will inject money into the business and be a professional triumph and create family unity. It's the fact that I'm never going to have to see that smug grin of yours again.'

Adam stopped suddenly on the stairs and turned around, a step below her so she was almost at eye level for once. 'You didn't seem to mind it a moment ago, when you thought I was going to kiss you,' he said, with a deadly accuracy that pierced her right in the gut.

'I was thinking of ways to let you down gently,' she lied. 'Or, failing that, to push you off the roof.'

He snorted. 'No, you weren't. You were thinking about how good it was going to be. That you know as well as I do that we have chemistry so strong that it's making it impossible to get any work done together. That you are terrified of going to Paris with me tomorrow because you don't know how you're going to resist me.'

She crossed her arms, determined that she wouldn't show him how many accurate statements he'd managed to pack into that one little speech.

'Tell me you don't really believe all of that,' she demanded.

'I know it because I feel it,' he said, leaning closer, right into her personal space. 'Because you've been the only distraction in my entire career that I can't seem to ignore.

Because I'm thinking about how close I'm going to be sitting to you on the flight tomorrow and wondering how I'm going to stop myself touching you. Because just as I was telling myself that I was pretending to kiss you to mess with you, the whole thing was playing out in my head and I've never wanted anything as badly as I wanted that kiss.'

She stared at him, unable to believe that he'd just offered all those secrets up. Made himself as vulnerable as he was asking her to be. More, because he'd gone first and she could turn around now and lie and tell him this was completely in his head and she could walk away from him without a second thought.

But she'd hesitated too long for that. Stared at him too long. Let her eyes sweep down his body, and back up to his face, and she was certain that every filthy thought she had about him on the way was written all over her face. What was the point of denying it when he already knew everything?

'So what do we do about it?' she asked, her voice so low it was nearly breaking.

'We've tried ignoring it,' he said.

She nodded. 'Didn't work.'

'Not for me.'

'Then I think the only thing we can do is go with it. We get this out of our system, now, before it gets in the way of our work any more than it already has.'

'And, just to be clear,' he said, and she took the strangled note in his voice as a win, 'when you say that we get this out of our systems…'

'I mean we do this the old-fashioned way. We bang it out so that I can stop thinking about you every second of the day and get the hell back to work.'

He stared at her for a full minute before he found his words. 'Fine. If that's what it's going to take. My office or yours?'

Instead of answering, Liv grabbed him by the shirt and shoved him against the wall, taking full advantage of the way the staircase evened out the difference in their height. She crushed his lips with hers, determined to win at least once tonight. He'd driven her to absolute distraction. Forced her to face the truth of how she felt about him, what she wanted, and now she was going to make him pay.

Except, he didn't seem to understand that this was a punishment. Because he groaned with pleasure and tightened his arms around her waist, pinning her tight against him. Then he was sliding his hands down her thighs, catching her behind her knees, lifting and turning at the same time so that she was the one against the wall now.

And he simply refused to meet her punishing pace, responding to her bruising kisses with tenderness, gentleness. Until he was going so slowly that she pulled her mouth away from his in frustration, pushing at his shoulder to get his attention.

'What the hell is this?' she asked.

'I thought we'd already talked about what this is.

'We never talked about being *nice*.'

He had the absolute balls to laugh at her. She was going to kill him, just as soon as she'd got what she wanted from him.

'I hate you,' she said again, which only made him laugh at her again. She tried not to react when he started trailing the lightest of kisses along her jaw. When his hands stroked along her thighs where they were locked around his waist. But she couldn't stifle the sound that escaped her when his fingers found the buttons at the front of her shirt and pinged them open, one by one. When she reached for his belt buckle, desperate to get what she wanted, to get this over with, he grasped her wrists and pinned them to the wall, then leaned back when she tried to kiss him again.

'You just want to torture me,' she accused, knowing that her expression was petulant.

'If you've got a problem, feel free to make a complaint to HR. Personally, I see no point in rushing,' Adam said. 'If we're going to do this, we're going to do it properly. I want you well and truly out of my system and that means being thorough. The torture's just a bonus.'

She groaned and let her head fall back against the wall, realising for the first time that the harder she pushed, the more he would resist her attempts to get this over with quickly.

'This is meant to be hate sex,' she reminded him as he walked them both towards his office, then cleared the papers from his desk with one sweep and dumped her unceremoniously on the edge of the table, so that she had to look up at him, feeling dishevelled and out of sorts, while he looked…

He looked so hot she didn't know what to do with herself. She knew that if she reached for his belt again, he'd only slow down further. So she leaned back on her hands, letting her shirt fall apart and reveal the silk and lace of her bra. He wanted torture? Fine. Two could play at that game. She glanced down at herself, teasing the edge of the lace with a fingertip, and then looked back up at his face, to make sure it was having the desired effect.

His jaw was so tense that she worried they'd be calling an emergency dentist before they left for Paris. Well, good. She had him exactly where she wanted him. She pushed her shirt off one shoulder and then the other, and, oh, would you look at that, one bra strap just happened to fall too, so that the top of her breast was offered up to him, and it would take the tiniest of nudges from him to reveal her hard nipple, just peeking from under the lace.

This time when she reached for his belt, he didn't try and stop her. In fact he held himself so deadly still that she knew that he was clinging onto self-control by the tiniest, most fragile of threads. She smirked to herself. She was going to break him, and afterwards she'd make him thank her for it.

'You look pretty pleased with yourself,' he observed from somewhere above her head, his voice strained.

She licked her lips, because she absolutely was pleased with herself, she thought as she tugged down his trousers and boxers and gasped an inbreath when Adam caught her wrists and leaned over her, so that she had no choice but to lean back, let him pin her hands to the wooden tabletop, feel his weight pressing her down. 'But you should know that I'm going to make you pay for that,' he said, before he crushed her mouth with a kiss.

He refused to break her gaze as he hooked an arm behind her knee, pulling her close. And all of her urgency fell away. Because she didn't want this to be rushed. She didn't want this to be over. If this was all they were going to have, she wanted it to last. Maybe for ever. This was so much better than fighting. This was so much better than winning. One of Adam's hands came to the side of her face and she turned her cheek into it, biting the inside of her mouth to cut through the intense wave of tenderness she felt for him at that moment.

'Okay?' he murmured, close to her ear, and she pressed her lips against his skin, savouring the taste of him, the closest to a 'yes' that she could manage while her mind was reeling and her body falling apart.

CHAPTER SEVEN

LIV'S THOUGHTS CAME back to her slowly as she tried to catch her breath, lying on the floor of Adam's office, looking up at the underside of his desk, not entirely sure how they had got here. Or, if that was meant to be a fight, whether she had won.

She sat up and looked around her, wondering what had happened to her bra. Eventually she spotted it hooked over the corner of the computer monitor, and her panties on the office chair, so she slid those on first and gradually started putting herself back together.

'Mmm...' Adam said, still lying on the floor, propping himself up on his elbow so that he could watch her. 'I guess we should get back to work.'

'If we don't, that was a complete waste of time,' she pointed out, trying to locate her usual bluster, but unable to resist a smile when he laughed at her. It was so much more difficult to be angry with him after they'd had sex. It wasn't the ideal working relationship, she had to admit. But from where she was sitting, it didn't seem so bad right now.

Probably, it would be simpler if that had been a little less good. If she had stuck to her guns and made him take her quickly against the wall in a stairwell rather than letting herself be lulled into…feelings and gentleness and what felt suspiciously like an emotional connection between them.

But that was just hormones messing with her head. Right now, she was bathed in endorphins, but she knew better than to mistake them for something real.

She sat in his office chair once she was dressed, as Adam was pulling on his trousers, and opened her laptop. There were only five hours before their flight, and this had to be finished. Adam took the seat opposite her without a word, which she refrained from mentioning because just because they'd had sex didn't mean they had to be all polite with one another. And she got back to work on their shared document.

They worked without speaking, their rapid-fire typing the only sound breaking the growing quiet of the night, glancing occasionally away from their screens to make eye contact over a snarky comment or deleted paragraph. But somehow, it worked. Their combined business experience, their completely polar-opposite life experiences. They complemented one another and challenged one another and created something that surpassed anything either of them had done alone.

Jonathan knocked on the door at six, and she glanced up at him, realising they had barely moved except for the odd bathroom or coffee break. He frowned, and then looked a little too knowing at the sight of her in Adam's seat.

'Everything okay here last night?' he asked. She made absolutely sure not to make eye contact with Adam, knowing that the briefest of glances would give them away.

'Fine, we're all done,' she said, shutting her laptop and faking a smile in her brother's direction. She glanced at her watch. 'With five minutes to spare before the car to the airport gets here.'

'Rowan asked me to give you this.' He

handed over her holdall, with everything that she would need for her night in Paris.

'Thanks,' she said, taking it from him. 'Was there something else?' she asked, as Jonathan hesitated in front of her.

'Just… I believe in you. You'll be great over there,' he said, somewhat awkwardly, and this time when she smiled at him, it was for real.

'Oh, Jonathan,' she said, swatting affectionately at his arm. 'Did you just have a feeling? Rowan's such a good influence on you.'

He looked heavenward and pinched his nose. 'Just go and don't make me regret it.'

She walked out of the office without looking at Adam but heard him exchanging a few words with Jonathan behind her. She stepped into the lift and turned to watch the two men. When Adam started to walk towards her, she planted her hands on her hips and let herself smile at him. As the doors started to close, she finally locked eyes with Adam's and grinned just as the doors closed with him on the other side of them.

'Well, that was childish,' Adam said when he caught up with her in the lobby after seemingly jogging down the stairs.

Liv flashed him an innocent smile. 'Just didn't want you thinking that I'd be a push-over now—'

'I've got my leg over.'

'You're so classy, Adam. That's what I like about you.'

'Get in the car.'

She glared at him as he opened the door for her and she slid into the back seat, conscious of not causing an argument in front of the staff who were starting to make their way into the building. Once the car door closed behind Adam, they fell into uncomfortable silence.

The silence held for an impressively long time. Through the car journey, into the airport, through the long security queues and right up until they were shown to business-class seats on the plane.

'I think there's been some sort of mistake,' Liv told the flight attendant.

'No, no mistake,' Adam said behind her, waving off the cabin crew with a smile. 'I upgraded us,' he said to Liv in a quiet voice, putting his carry-on into the overhead locker and holding out his hand for her case.

She stubbornly held on to it. She wasn't

handing over anything without answers. 'Kinley is in the middle of a cost-saving exercise, and you organise an upgrade without even speaking to me about it?'

'I paid for the tickets,'

Liv snorted, amused. 'I'm the spoiled princess but you're the one who can't face a flight to Paris in economy? It's only an hour, Adam.'

He took a step towards her, so his voice barely had to be more than a whisper for her to hear him.

'And do you want your thigh pressed against mine for an hour without being able to touch? You'd have dragged me into the bathroom before we were even over the channel.'

Liv looked up at him, considering. Then lifted a hand to his cheek and pulled his head down so she could whisper into his ear.

'As if you'd make it to the bathroom.'

He pulled Liv's bag from her hand, shoved it roughly into the overhead locker, then steered Liv into her seat with a hand on each of her hips. He pinned her there with a stare while he fastened her seat belt and then crossed his arms and leaned back to look at her.

'It really scares you that much?' Liv asked. 'What you feel for me?'

Adam wasn't sure what it was that hit him in the gut—Liv's words, or his own realisation that they were true. She did scare him. The chemistry between them scared him. The fact that sleeping together had made things a thousand times worse scared him.

Because they couldn't take that back. He had thought that it was hard being near to her when the sexual chemistry was all about the unknown. When he had been permanently distracted, wondering what it would be like if she let down those barriers for a minute. Wondering what she tasted like. How she would sound.

Having the answer to those questions was meant to stop him wondering. Stop him being distracted. He was meant to be concentrating right now on the meeting they were flying to. Not indulging himself in a frame-by-frame replay of what had happened in his office that morning. How was he ever going to get any work done on that desk again? But Jonathan had seen them in there. It would be way too obvious to start switching out furniture, or suddenly deciding that he'd rather hot desk.

He returned from the bathroom to find

Liv still in her seat, though she had undone her lap belt.

'Are you feeling better after your caveman act?' she asked with her brows raised as he sat down beside her. He gritted his teeth and resisted the urge to snap at her. That was exactly what she wanted, so he had to refuse to give it to her.

He had to find a way to undo the damage that they had done the night before. Had to forget all the things that they had learnt about one another. It was only as the adrenaline buzz of their all-nighter was wearing off that he was realising how stupid he had been to think that this was something that he could get out of his system and then move on from.

He wondered whether she felt the same. Or if she'd forgotten it already. Perhaps she'd got him out of her system, just as they had planned. He had to know. He glanced across at her. She was staring out of the window, looking for all the world as if she were relaxed and carefree. But he wasn't all the world. He knew her more intimately than that. He only had to close his eyes and he could kiss her. Smell her. Taste her. And when he looked at her staring out of the window, he also saw the way that she tangled her fingers together. The tension in her shoulders that kept her turned away from him. She was anything but unaffected. Well, that could only make things worse.

This trip would be a challenge. There was no doubt about it. It would be stupid to think that he didn't have to be on his guard if they weren't going to end up back exactly where they were the night before. He knew that he would be tempted. He knew that he could talk himself into it again. That it was *logical* and *sensible* and that he was doing it for *reasons* rather than because he wanted her so desperately that he couldn't resist her for a moment longer.

He couldn't allow himself to get any more involved with her than he already was. He knew that relationships only worked if you were prepared to be vulnerable, and he had learned early on that being tough was how he'd survived. How he and his mother had dragged themselves out of poverty and homelessness. He had finally found stability. Security. And he wasn't prepared to jeopardise that by introducing an element as disruptive as Livia Kinley.

The business-class seats did their job, and he was able to get through the whole flight without touching Liv—accidentally or otherwise—and thank God Liv seemed as determined to stay away from him as he was from her.

By the time that they were checking into their hotel, he had been lulled into a false sense of security. So when they reached the reception desk, and the receptionist's brows knitted together, he was instantly back on his guard.

'Is there a problem?' he asked as the receptionist clicked through different pages.

'Are you certain you booked two rooms?' she asked in lightly accented English.

'Yes!' they both said with such force that she looked up at them in surprise.

'I have both your names assigned to a double room at present, but—'

'No. That is unacceptable,' Adam said.

At the same time as Liv declared, 'Absolutely not. Find us another room. I don't care how you do it.' Liv didn't want to know what their expressions were showing to make the receptionist have to try hard, as she clearly was, to hide her smile.

'Well, I have no regular rooms, but I

would be happy to upgrade you to a suite at our expense. Would that be acceptable?'

'Separate bedrooms?' Liv and Adam both asked together, making the receptionist smile at them properly this time.

'Separate bedrooms,' she confirmed. 'And a shared living and dining space.'

'That's fine,' Liv said. 'Thank you.'

'My apologies for the confusion with the booking. I hope it won't affect the rest of your stay.'

Adam nodded, his jaw tight. 'I'm sure it won't.'

They followed her directions up to the suite, and when they felt the door close behind them, she felt the tension ramp up.

'Was the universe trying to interfere?' Liv asked as she set down her bag.

'Just an administrative error,' Adam said, rubbing his hand over his jaw. 'It doesn't mean anything. And it's fixed now anyway.'

'Right,' Liv said, crossing to one of the doors, and finding behind it a bedroom with a view of the Eiffel Tower.

'Shotgun this room,' she called over her

shoulder. She walked to the huge windows and looked across the city to the tower.

'Whatever you want, Princess,' Adam called back to her.

She smiled to herself because his jibes didn't sting any more. Instead, they did something much more dangerous. They warmed her, sparked memories of the night before, which couldn't be anything other than a mistake. They'd dodged one attempt by the universe—or the hotel's booking system—to try and throw them back into the same bed. Now they just had to get through the rest of this trip without doing something as stupid as they had done the night before. Because it didn't matter how they tried to justify it, last night had been a stupid idea. Had either of them genuinely believed that sex would make their chemistry better, rather than worse? Or, as she was realising now, had he simply used that excuse to take something that he'd wanted, regardless of the fact that it was dangerous?

Well, at least they wouldn't be able to fool themselves with that logic again. Because they could be in no doubt this morning that they absolutely had not got it out of their systems. If the way Adam had turned away from her on the plane was anything to go by, his body was as up for round two as hers was. They were relying on their better judgement now to keep that from happening.

She pulled her laptop from her bag and got it set up at the dressing table in her bedroom. There was nothing like work to keep her mind occupied.

The master parfumier they were meeting with later today worked with only a select few clients each year, and had told Livia on the phone that he absolutely did not have room in his schedule to create a signature fragrance for the house of Kinley.

But he was the great-grandson of the parfumier who had created the original Kinley fragrance for her great-grandmother, and there was no chance that Liv would be leaving Paris until she'd convinced him to update his great-grandfather's vision for the twenty-first century. They had a shared history. A shared story, and Liv wasn't going to be shy about leaning on that family connection if it meant that this meeting was going to go the way she wanted it.

'Are you ready to go?' Adam asked, knocking on her door an hour later—she'd showered, changed into a smart black shift dress and given her briefing document one last read-through. If she wasn't ready now, she wasn't sure when she would be.

Which was when she made the mistake of looking up at Adam, waiting for her in the doorway of her room. Ever since she'd met him, he'd lived in a uniform of jeans, black T-shirt. That leather jacket she wanted to steal. They were on their way to a meeting. She'd got changed. It shouldn't have surprised her that he'd swapped his casual clothes for a suit. But then, the effect shouldn't have been so devastating. It was only a suit, but it was such an unexpected look on him that she couldn't help staring. Not too long ago he would have liked that, she knew. Would have liked having that power over her. But not now that he knew what they were like together.

'It's just a suit,' he said with a scowl, and she looked deliberately away from him, angry at herself for being so transparent.

But as she slid her feet into her patent black stilettos, she could feel his eyes on her, and he didn't look away until she shrugged on her cream wool coat and grabbed her bags and her papers.

It was a short walk to the parfumier's, and it was a relief to finally reach his office and allow the presence of other people to pierce the tension between her and Adam.

They were shown into a stylish room adjoining Monsieur Gaspard's office and she crossed her ankles neatly to stop herself from fidgeting. When the door to his office opened and Claude Gaspard stepped out, she couldn't help her eyes widening. What was it with beautiful men in suits in this city? He was as tall as Adam, with warm brown skin, close-cropped hair and wide, dark eyes.

But she wasn't here to look at either of the men in the room, she was here to work. She shook Gaspard's hand and then kissed him on both cheeks for good measure. 'Thanks so much for seeing us at late notice, Monsieur Gaspard,' she said. 'This is Adam Jackson. He's working with us on the launch.'

'A pleasure,' Gaspard replied. 'Please call me Claude. My great-grandfather would never have forgiven me if I'd not made time to speak with Madame Kinley's great-granddaughter.'

Liv smiled. 'Liv, please. I found their let-ters, you know. It seemed as if they were great friends. I think she would have been so pleased to know that their vision would finally become reality.'

'Ah, well,' Gaspard said with a laugh. 'I knew you were here to try and convince me to change our entire schedule for the next year. I suppose I should hear your pitch be-fore I have to give you disappointing news.'

Gaspard smiled at Livia and gestured with a sweeping arm for her to precede him into the office. Adam followed them in and tamped down the urge to glower. Gaspard hadn't been flirting, he had been friendly, he told himself. Not that there would be anything wrong with him flirting with Livia. Adam had absolutely no justification for the surge of jealousy he felt in his chest at the idea.

He wasn't here being all jealous of some guy Liv had only just met. Who she was charming because she wanted to work with, not because she wanted to date. Anyway, he wasn't the jealous type, and he had no claim over Liv. They'd wanted to get each other out of their systems. That was why last night had happened. If she wanted to do the same with

the wealthy, cultured, good-looking French-
man who was smiling at her from across the
desk, that was none of his business. So why
did the thought of it make his fists clench
until his finger muscles were stiff?

It had been his intention to take charge
and lead this meeting. He hadn't even
wanted Liv to be there. But she was on a
roll, talking through their plans with such
enthusiasm that Gaspard was hanging on her
every word. He could have interrupted and
steered attention in his own direction, but
he couldn't think of a good reason to inter-
rupt when she was doing just as good a job
as he would have been.

She was talking schedules now, which
had always been the sticking point with
Gaspard. This had been the whole reason
he had flown out for this meeting. But sitting watching Liv talk him round, he realised that she had this. In the end, he just
sat back and enjoyed watching her work.
She went heavy on heritage, the shared history of their two companies, something he
would never have been able to pull off. The
experience that he'd built up over the last de-
cade counted for nothing alongside people

whose great-grandparents had done business together.

Eventually Gaspard held up his hands with a smile and a laugh. 'Okay, okay, you have convinced me what a wonderful partnership this would be, and I have committed to trying—' at this point Liv gave him a hard stare '—to *trying* to find a way to make your schedule work. Now, it is my duty, as you are a visitor to my city, that I ask if you would like to have dinner with me tonight.'

Adam froze, wondering how Liv would react. Because, no matter how professionally his invitation was worded, it was painfully obvious that he was asking her on a date. Liv's shoulders stiffened slightly and he knew that she was aware of it too. He held himself utterly still beside her, wondering what she was going to say. In the end, when she smiled, he recognised that it was slightly strained. 'That's a very kind offer but I have a lot of work to do this evening. I'm excited to visit the laboratory tomorrow and I want to think over everything we've talked about today.'

Gaspard smiled at Liv magnanimously, accepting her gentle brush-off at face value.

'Of course,' he said. 'Perhaps next time you are in the city.'

'Perhaps,' Liv agreed, standing and offering her hand across the desk. Adam noted the lack of cheek-kisses this time, and then berated himself for noticing. There was absolutely no reason for him to notice or care whether Liv observed English or French social conventions at the end of their meeting.

He avoided making eye contact as he shook hands with Gaspard and they were shown out of the building. Light flooded the avenue as they exited onto the street, and Liv turned to look up at him with a beaming smile. 'I think he's going to do it,' she said.

'I think there was a point in that meeting when he would have given you anything that you asked for.'

'What's that supposed to mean?'

She stopped and glared at him, stepping in front of him with a hand on his chest so that he couldn't ignore her.

'Nothing. I'm sorry, I shouldn't have said anything,' Adam said, trying to sidestep around her. But she stepped in front of him again.

'No. Tell me what you meant.'

He hesitated, but then the words burst out of him, uninvited. 'He asked you out.'

'He was just being polite,' she countered. 'I'm sure the invitation included you too.'

He had to laugh. 'I'm absolutely certain that it didn't, and I think you know that too.' She shrugged his comment off, turned around and carried on walking back to their hotel.

'I'm not going to apologise for him asking me out.'

'I never asked you to. Why would I even expect that? It's nothing to me if you go out with him.'

Liv snorted, which really irritated him. 'Really, it's nothing to you if the girl you had sex with last night agrees to a date with a gorgeous French guy right in front of you? Sure, you're a very cool customer.'

Adam forced himself to shrug, though he was sure that it looked stiff and unnatural. 'We both agreed that it didn't mean anything. If you wanted to go to dinner with him, you could have said yes.'

'I know that I *could have* said yes. I didn't need your permission, but I didn't want to! Why would I want to go out with him when last ni—?' Liv stopped, cutting herself off. 'We've got completely off track,' she said after a long deep breath. 'I didn't want or expect him to ask me out. I didn't want to go so I said no.'

Adam put a hand to her shoulder, and she stopped as soon as he touched her. 'I'm sorry,' he said, really meaning it. 'I was just being…'

'Jealous and annoying?'

His instinct was to deny it, but he couldn't. He *was* jealous, and Liv knew it, and it was pointless to deny it.

'You're right. I was jealous. I know it doesn't make any sense.' It was surely just some lizard-brain, caveman response to sleeping together. That was all this feeling was. Right now he'd ignore the fact that he'd had sex plenty of times without getting attached before. Without ever feeling jealous.

It didn't mean anything because he wouldn't let it mean anything. All he had to do—*all* he had to do—was not have sex with Livia again. That really shouldn't feel like as difficult a prospect as it currently did.

'So you wouldn't really have been okay if I had gone to dinner with him?'

Somehow honesty seemed to work between them. Burying their feelings only made them more potent. So he told the truth. 'I would have been gutted if you'd gone out with him,' he said.

'Good, because if the roles had been reversed, I would have scratched their eyes out.'

He tried not to let his smile show, but could feel his mouth twitch at the corner. 'Well, I'm not going out to dinner with Gaspard,' she said, 'and it would be too tragic to get a table for one in Paris, so are we going to eat together tonight?'

'Working dinner with room service?'

She shook her head. 'We barely stopped for dinner last night. We've earned a couple of hours off.'

'You told Gaspard—'

'I know what I told him. Anyway, I'm not sure that dinner in our room is a good idea.'

Adam smirked at her. 'Afraid you won't be able to resist me?' Liv didn't smile back.

She looked at him seriously, enough of a change of tone to make him break his stride. 'What?' he asked.

'Do you think it worked?' she said, and he

couldn't be sure what she meant. Couldn't answer her if he couldn't be sure what she was asking. 'Do you think we got each other out of our systems?' she asked, catching her bottom lip between her teeth, showing her discomfort.

Selfishly, he wanted her to go first. Not to have to be the one to expose their vulnerabilities. But she had asked the question, and they had been intimate enough that he felt he owed her honesty, if nothing else.

'I don't think it did. Not for me at least,' he confessed. 'I want you just as much as I did before. More, probably.'

She listened to him in silence, leaving him desperate to know what she was thinking. Was she going to come out and tell him that this was completely one-sided now? He drew in his emotional armour, getting ready to front this out if it turned out that he'd just made a huge mistake.

'It didn't for me either,' she admitted with a groan. 'And I hate how much I liked you being jealous.'

'That's bad,' Adam acknowledged.

'You don't have to tell me that,' she said as they reached the hotel, stopped briefly at reception to ask for coffee to be sent up, and then took the old cage elevator up to their suite.

'So what do we do about this?' Liv asked, as she kicked off her heels and dropped onto a couch. 'Ignoring our attraction to one another didn't work, and we've tried getting it out of our systems but that didn't work either. I don't know what else we can try.'

'Well,' Adam said, sitting beside her and leaning forwards, his elbows resting on his knees. 'Really there are only two options…'

She looked up at him, her expression urging him to go on.

'We either have sex again or we don't,' he said, and Liv laughed at his bluntness.

'I guess that's what it comes down to,' she agreed.

'We've tested both options already,' Adam went on, 'so the question isn't what does each achieve—because we already know that they both lead to the same place: to wanting one another. So that leaves us with the risks to evaluate.'

'I can't believe you're subjecting our…' She paused, and he waited for her to finish her sentence and define whatever this was that they were doing here. 'Whatever,' she finished, wimping out of giving this any kind of name. 'I can't believe you're doing a SWOT analysis to decide if we should have sex again.'

'Do you have a better idea?' Adam asked, and she shook her head.

'I'm so embarrassed that I don't. Business school nerds are the worst.'

'So if we don't have another idea, let's do the analysis. Having sex. What are the threats? Go.'

Liv thought for a moment. 'You fall madly in love with me, get too attached and make things awkward when I break your heart.'

Adam snorted. 'Somehow, I think I'll survive. But you make a good point. Once wasn't enough. What's to say twice would be? Or three times? Four?'

'So the biggest threat involved with having more sex is…wanting more sex?'

'Honestly you're not making it sound that threatening.'

'So come up with something else. There have to be other good reasons not to do this.'

'It could distract us from our work. Ruin things with Gaspard.'

'I'm a professional. I'm not that easily distracted. You have a very high opinion of how good you are at sex.'

'You think I couldn't distract you from your work?' Adam asked, with a dangerous smirk. 'We're doing a SWOT analysis on our affair right now rather than something more productive and you haven't even seen me naked yet.'

Liv groaned. 'Don't talk about being naked when we're trying to make good decisions. Think of another reason not to do this.'

'Your brother might kill me?' he suggested, which made Liv roll her eyes.

'I don't care about that.'

'Babe. You're really not helping,' Adam pointed out.

'Nor is calling me babe. I don't like it.'

That got one of his proper smiles. 'Why do you think I keep doing it?'

'I hate you,' Liv declared with a melodramatic sigh, leaning back on the couch with a hand over her face.

'That seems like it would be a good enough reason not to have sex with me,' Adam pointed out. She pulled her hand away and narrowed her eyes at him.

'You'd think so, wouldn't you?'

'So we've got…nothing?' he asked, his elbows on his thighs.

'The worst we've got is that it'll make us want more sex—not an effective deterrent—or that we'll end up liking each other, which is just not realistic.'

'So, we should just go with it?' he asked.

She shrugged. 'As long as we don't bring feelings into it, I can't see what harm it could do.'

'You really need to work on your sweet-talking game.'

'If you don't like it, feel free to walk away. You'd be doing us both a favour.'

He stood from the couch, and for a moment she wondered whether he was going to take her up on her suggestion and walk away. Instead, he came to stand directly in front of her, nudging her knees apart until he was between her thighs. She let out a shaky breath as she looked up and met his gaze, which was more intense than she had ever seen it.

Adam held out his hand to her, and her palm was in his before she had even decided to do it. When he pulled her to stand he was close, too close, and she had no choice but to let him help take her weight if she didn't want to topple backwards. Adam wrapped his arms around her waist, and hers came up around his neck. She knew what came next; she could feel Adam's breath on her lips. She wasn't quite sure why they weren't kissing already. Why she wasn't kissing him. All she knew was that brushing her lips on his was putting everything on the line. She caught her lip between her teeth instead, wondering if it was too late to back out now. Oh, she had no worries about Adam pressing her to do something she didn't want to. It was her own judgement, her own self-control that she couldn't trust.

Kissing Adam when they'd both agreed it was a one-off was one thing. But this had suddenly become frighteningly open-ended, and the stakes were maybe too high.

But this was just stalling because as intimidating as this was, it was also inevitable. She'd spent the last twelve hours not kissing Adam and she knew that her resolve was running on fumes. This was going to happen. The only questions were how, and how much it was going to cost her.

Not getting emotionally involved had never been a problem before. Once she'd been abandoned by her parents—the very definition of having your heart broken—it had become second nature to keep her feelings out of her relationships. What was the point of putting your heart on the line when you had unequivocal proof of how easy you were to leave? She would have to be a masochist to start something knowing how bad it hurt when the person you loved didn't love you back.

Rowan had been the exception. Whatever benevolent higher power had engineered them sharing a flat at university had been her saviour. She hadn't *let* herself love Rowan, it had just happened, slowly, over time. It had snuck up on her without her realising it was something that she should have been guarding against. It had never occurred to her that Rowan could break her heart. Until she had fallen in love with Jonathan. Oh, Liv was pleased that they were happy, of course. But Rowan had been *hers*. She'd been the person she'd relied on most since her parents had left. And now? Rowan had promised Liv that nothing would change. But how could that be true? She would put Jonathan first now. Liv knew how selfish it made her to even think that. But she couldn't help it.

Adam tucked a strand of hair behind her ear and gifted her with a smile.

'I don't think your heart's in this,' he said, his hand cupping her cheek. 'Please tell me you're thinking better of this and you're going to save us from ourselves.'

She gave herself a mental slap on the forehead. This was Adam she was talking about. He'd made himself absolutely clear that he didn't want anything more than sex. There couldn't be a safer man to have a series of one-nighters with and then leave. It was the most honest she had ever been going into a relationship. So, finally, she pulled him down, pressed her lips on his, and gave herself permission to stop thinking. Let Adam do the thinking. He was never going to give her any reason to think that this was more than it was. And that would keep her safe too. All they had to do was keep this about the sex, and not let feelings creep in at the edges.

CHAPTER EIGHT

Liv DROPPED BACK on her pillow, trying to catch her breath, trying not to think how embarrassing it would be to die in a foreign hotel room of too much sex. She glanced across at Adam, who had hit the pillow next to her, his skin shiny from sweat, chest heaving as he tried to catch his breath.

'I need some air,' Liv said, pulling the sheet off her bed and wrapping it around her as she crossed to the curtains and the balcony beyond. She drew back the drapes and gasped. She'd somehow forgotten that she'd selected this room for its view. The light show from the Eiffel Tower spilt into the room and she followed its path to her bed, where Adam was stretched out, entirely unabashed by the fact that her theft of the sheet had left him naked. He'd stretched one arm up behind his head, and, despite the hours they had just spent in her bed, there was still heat in his eyes.

'I'm starving,' she said, and Adam smirked. She rolled her eyes. 'For food,' she clarified, whacking him on the chest. 'Don't be so predictable. I need to eat something.'

'Room service?' Adam asked as she stepped back towards the bed.

'I don't trust you not to get distracted,' she replied, finding a robe on the back of the bathroom door and throwing it at him. 'Put some clothes on,' she told him, and then stepped back in the bathroom to turn on the shower. 'I'm taking you out for dinner.'

Adam let the shower wash the scent of Livia from him, his skin stinging from the water pressure.

There was no point in second-guessing their decision to go to bed together. An altogether different experience from his desk, or the floor of his office. It had been inevitable. Had felt that way since the minute that he'd met her. She was less distracting when they weren't trying to pretend not to see something that was right in front of them.

And he didn't need to worry about getting

too involved. She had made it perfectly clear that she was no more interested in that than he himself was. And dinner? It wasn't as if it were a date. She was right: they both needed to refuel, and that was unlikely to happen if they didn't leave their suite.

He was still pulling his T-shirt over his head when he walked into their living area. She was in jeans, trainers, a white T-shirt knotted and revealing a strip of skin at her waist. He hadn't realised how much he'd needed to see that she wasn't treating this like a date. Her still-damp hair was scraped back into a high ponytail, her face free of make-up, and his gaze caught on the freckles across her cheekbones, the bridge of her nose. The sight made him want to drag her back to bed, pin her to the mattress until he'd made a thorough survey and kissed every one of them.

'Ready to go?' she asked, an inquisitive expression on her face. His brain stumbled a moment, realising how distracted he'd let himself get.

'Yeah, ready,' he replied, pulling on his shoes and grabbing keys and his phone from the table. They both turned to the stairs rather than the lift, keeping moving, avoiding the forced intimacy of that enclosed space. They shouldn't need to take such measures now that they'd decided to stop fighting their attraction. But sex wasn't the same thing as intimacy. It was good that they were being cautious right now. These post-coital, endorphin-flooded moments were the most dangerous. It would be too easy to let their hands brush together, to twine their fingers. To set a pattern that would blur the lines between what this thing was, and what it wasn't.

They paused outside the hotel restaurant downstairs, and Adam raised his eyebrows. It was atmospherically lit, and from the lobby he could see crisp white tablecloths and candles glinting on crystal. It was the very picture of Parisian romance. He risked a look at Liv, who was looking slightly green beside him. 'Walk and find somewhere else?' she suggested.

'God, yes,' he said, letting out a breath.

'What's with you?' she asked. 'How can you be so tense?' They walked out onto the street, a wide, elegant boulevard, and turned towards the river. 'I feel like I'm made of noodles.'

Adam smiled. His smug feeling of self-satisfaction was entirely involuntary. Liv was right, though. He was tense. He could feel his shoulders up somewhere around his ears. They reached the river and stopped, leaning on the balustrade, watching the water. He took a couple of deep breaths and let his shoulders fall.

'There's a lot riding on this trip,' he said. Liv nodded, and he thought he might just get away with that obfuscation.

'So you're not freaking out about the fact that we had sex and then were immediately faced with one of the most romantic cities in the world? And now you're not wondering if I meant it when I said I wanted this to be casual and you're spiralling and wondering how you're going to get out of this without breaking my tender female heart?'

Adam laughed, turning away from the water and leaning back, looking across at her.

'I think at the moment I'm mostly worrying about how you can read me like a book.'

'Well, stop worrying. And stop with the brooding expression. It's making me want to kiss it off you, and my tender female heart is still absolutely starving.'

'Fine, fine,' he said, pushing away from the wall and grabbing her hand to pull her with him. They were halfway to the bar on the corner before he realised what he'd done. It was nothing. Just a casual gesture to ensure that they were walking in the same direction. He fought down the urge to flex his fingers, knowing it would only draw her attention, make her think that he thought it was a big deal. Something other than a completely unremarkable gesture.

When they reached the bar—loud, lively, not in the least romantic—he dropped her hand and reached for the door. He reached past her and pushed the door open in front of her. They pulled up stools at the bar, and Liv looked through the wine list before ordering herself a glass. Adam ordered himself a beer and they both ordered food. They could eat right here at the bar, the furthest thing from a romantic dinner for two that he could imagine.

He should be sated, he thought. He'd had more sex than he'd had in a year. A rare steak and a cold beer. They'd had a good meeting that morning, with the promise of another tomorrow. There was really no reason he could think of for this mild sense of dissatisfaction in his chest. It was because they hadn't slept the night before. He was tired. That was all.

'Ready to call it a night?' Liv asked, as the music slowed. Their plates had been cleared, their glasses refilled. The atmosphere was edging closer to intimate, and Adam was looking as if he needed to bolt.

It was adorable, she thought, how utterly terrified he seemed. As if, if he wasn't careful, feelings were somehow going to sneak up on him and bite him. If he wasn't constantly vigilant.

'Time to go,' Liv suggested, and Adam practically sprang from his seat.

'Yeah, if you want,' he said, as if the thought had only just occurred to him and he hadn't been glancing at the door every thirty seconds for the past ten minutes.

'You're twitchy,' she commented as they walked back towards the hotel. 'It's giving me a complex.'

'It's not you, it's me,' Adam said, forcing an eyebrow raise from Liv. 'I'm generally not great at the whole talking thing. "*I had a difficult childhood, blah-blah-blah...*" This just feels...unsettling. I wasn't expecting it. And in my life, unexpected and unsettling has never led anywhere good. Feeling like I don't know what is round the corner—I don't know. I guess it's tapped into something.'

She bumped her side against his. 'You don't need to feel unsettled. You can just ask me what's going on if you feel like you don't know.'

He gave her a weak smile. 'I know. And you've already told me what you want. It's not about that.'

'Then what is it about?'

'I don't know. I'm not used to feeling like this. Like I've had too much of you and like I can't get enough. Like I need you.'

She frowned as they walked along, doing her best to understand. 'And needing someone is a bad thing?' she asked. 'Set aside the fact that it's me, for a moment. Let's just talk hypothetically.'

Adam nodded. 'Needing *anything* is a problem when you can't be certain you're going to be able to get it,' he explained. 'We, I, *people* already have enough needs: something to eat, somewhere to sleep, some way of keeping warm. Hope—a way out and a plan to get all of those things.'

Liv was starting to understand, and it made her ache for all he had suffered. Not that she could ever tell him that, of course. 'And what about someone to care about?' she asked. 'To care about you?'

Adam shook his head. 'I have that. I have my mum. She's been the one constant whatever was going on in my life. I have unconditional love from her, because she's been through it. Seen it all. I can't expect that from anyone else. I can't let myself want something when it's out of my control.'

Which made sense of why he was so jumpy at even the thought of an emotional connection with her. It was lucky for him, for both of them, that they were both as messed up as each other. That simple fact— the fact that they had both been irreparably damaged—was what was going to make this work.

'And here I am avoiding intimacy because the people who were meant to love me unconditionally didn't. We're a pair.' She forced a smile, because what else could you do?

'Mutually hopeless,' Adam agreed.

'Well, maybe that's a good thing,' Liv mused. 'Surely two such messed-up people can manage a short affair without it turning into something more serious.'

Adam nodded, and she felt something unclench inside her, some part of her she hadn't realised had been terrified that he was going to end this. 'I promise if I see you getting even remotely attached, I'll get rid of you.'

She laughed, but it sounded a little forced. 'Do you want to go straight back, or go for a walk?' Adam asked, changing the subject. 'We've seen barely anything of the city. It'd be a shame to go back to London having seen nothing but the inside of the hotel.'

'Oh, I don't know, I think I'm going to have fond memories of that particular hotel.' Adam grinned, and she couldn't help smiling back. 'Do you ever think we might be in trouble if a moonlit walk in Paris is the safer option?' Liv asked as they reached the Eiffel Tower.

She walked close to the tower, looked up so the gridded ironwork was a dark silhouette against the sky. Around her, she was aware that everyone else was hand in hand—or taking loved-up selfies—and she begged the universe not to let anyone drop to one knee and propose, drawing further attention to the fact that this was one of the most romantic spots on the planet. But the universe held, and the other couples drifted away leaving her and Adam alone.

'You're a nice guy,' she felt compelled to say, in an awkward moment of silence. Then she turned to look at him, mortified at what she'd just said. His gaze was fixed ahead and only the ticcing muscle in his jaw gave away that he'd heard her at all. She could see how nervous he was about what she was going to say, as if she were going to force him to have some feelings. She hid her smile.

'I'm just saying. You're an okay guy and if you met a girl less messed up than I am, you would probably make someone an okay, you know, guy.'

He glanced sideways, clearly still perturbed.

'God, that's it,' Liv said. 'Would you stop looking at me like I'm trying to trap you or something? Shall we just go back to the hotel and have sex now?'

He grinned, the relief coming off him in waves.

'God, yes. Let's go.'

They walked away from the tower side by side, and when his arm looped around her shoulders it felt friendly, not anything scarier. And it was friendly when they came through the door to their suite and he reached past her waist to lock the door. It was very friendly when she found herself caged by his arms with his hands resting on the door either side of her head, one thigh pressed between her legs, nudging her knees apart, and she knew he was teasing her, waiting for her to snap and turn this from something sweet into something fiery and fast and hard. But they'd done that. Several times, and she hated to repeat herself.

So she waited, wondering what else they could come up with, but the drawn-out tension of the moment curled in her chest as her ankle curled gently around Adam's calf, and she let her head fall to one side. If Adam wanted to go slow, then she was going to see what it felt like to be okay with that. What would she learn about him, about herself, if she didn't follow her usual playbook and allowed this to go somewhere different? It was still just sex. Just a different tempo than she was used to.

Adam lifted her and moved them through to her bedroom, and neither of them broke away to pull the drapes. And so when his mouth moved against hers in time with his body, he had reflected lights from passing cars across his bare shoulders. When she turned her head towards the window, unable to take the sweetness she saw in his expression, she could follow the lights on the tower where they had been standing a couple of hours before, when she had told him he was a nice guy, and not realised how dangerous that made him. Now she knew that she had been wrong, he wasn't just nice. He was achingly sweet. Gentle, now that she wasn't making him fight her for every concession.

It was too late to protect herself now, when he had drawn out everything she had to give and had made her beg him to take even more. His eyes met hers, and she felt the echo of her own feelings in his body as something passed between them, something intangible that twisted in her chest and tied her to him.

This was why she'd resisted, before. Why she always took control, took what she wanted. Because when she was calling the shots she could always be sure that she wouldn't be asked for more than she could give. That was why she'd pushed him against the wall and kissed him so hard that she couldn't think. Because that was safer than this. Safer than feeling something shift in your chest and knowing what you were doing couldn't be undone. Knowing that you wanted more and wouldn't be able to stop yourself taking it.

With anyone else, she would have squeezed her eyes shut. She would have made a joke and flipped the guy on his back and have taken control again. But when Adam's wide brown eyes met hers, looking every bit as surprised and scared as she did, she couldn't do that to him. Couldn't leave him alone with whatever it was he was feeling. So she pressed her cheek more deeply into the palm that cupped it, and clutched Adam tighter to her with a hand in his hair, and the other at the small of his back, so that there wasn't even a breath of air between their bodies.

She held on for countless minutes afterwards, when Adam gasped heavily into her neck, and she could only guess that he was as shell-shocked as she was, and breaking away, talking, looking him in the eye would make that real. And if it was real, she would have to run.

CHAPTER NINE

THEY'D FORGOTTEN TO draw the curtains, Adam thought with a slow smile, as morning sunlight turned his eyelids pink. If it weren't for the daylight that had woken him, they could pretend that last night wasn't over.

He reached an arm out across the bed and felt a stab of panic when he realised that Livia was gone. He sat abruptly, pulling back the sheets, as if somehow she could be under there. He forced himself to take a couple of breaths to calm his heartbeat. It was fine. There was nothing wrong, this was never going to be the sort of thing that involved long, lazy mornings in bed. There was no reason to have felt anything other than a mild 'huh' when he'd realised that he was alone. Which was why his reaction scared him so much. Because somehow between arriving back at the hotel last night and waking up this morning, something had shifted inside him, and now his body no longer just liked being close to Livia, it expected it. Needed it.

He should be grateful that she wasn't here—that he'd had this opportunity to see what was happening and put a stop to it. If he even needed to. Because Liv wasn't here—did that mean that she'd already had the same freak-out that he was currently experiencing and had done the right thing for both of them and scarpered?

He should be grateful, but instead he was mildly irritated, sorry for the loss of this morning before he had to face reality and put some distance between them. Where was Liv anyway? The suite was nice, but not so large that you could lose a person in it. Even one as neatly packaged as Liv. And he was in her room. Had she left right after he'd fallen asleep—unable to bear the thought of sharing a bed with him? If she had, he couldn't decide if he was more annoyed or pleased that she'd stolen the signature move from his playbook.

He pulled the sheet around him and looked around for his clothes. He found his boxers kicked over by the dressing table and pulled them on. A quick glance in the bathroom confirmed that Livia wasn't in the shower, so he took a deep breath and opened the door into their shared living space. Livia was sitting at their dining table, croissant in hand, papers and her laptop scattered around her. 'Good morning, sleeping beauty,' she said, with a smile that seemed as if she was genuinely pleased to see him until she tamped it down to make it something more careful and polite.

'How long have you been up?' Adam asked, taking note of the empty coffee pot in front of her, and the bouncing of her toe. She was ready for their meeting in another smart dress, with her hair shiny and dried in neat waves that made him want to run his hands through it until she looked like his again. No, not his. He didn't *do* possessive. He didn't do jealous. He definitely didn't do being crestfallen at waking up alone and feeling as if he wanted to demand an explanation. To draw her close to his body until the unquiet, insistent part of his chest settled at having her near.

He should just stick with his tried and tested morning-after routine, grab a quick shower to wash away the memories and any residual feelings and carry on with his day as if nothing had happened.

'I was starving,' Livia said, not looking up at him, her eyes on her laptop, and he fought down the urge to turn her face up to his and make her meet his eye. He didn't know what had got into him that morning. Only that he was grateful that she was more together than he was. Maybe it was because she'd already started on the caffeine. He'd feel himself again once he'd had a coffee.

'There's food,' she said, gesturing at the plates under silver cloches. 'But I finished the coffee. Go for a shower and I'll order some more.'

Adam crossed towards his own bedroom, with only a grunt as an answer—safer than words—and realised belatedly that he was still only wearing boxers. But it didn't matter, he supposed, if she wasn't going to look up from her work and acknowledge his existence. The fact that she wouldn't stung somewhere that hadn't existed before last night.

Livia rubbed the heels of her hands into her eye sockets before she looked up at the door that Adam had just closed slightly more firmly than was necessary. Perhaps the wind had caught it. Though she hadn't got around to opening any of the windows, or the door out onto the balcony.

So she had to assume that he was annoyed at her about something. Had he guessed the thoughts she'd been incapable of fighting off last night? He couldn't know, could he? She was certain that he didn't know how she'd stared at him in the half-light that morning, her eyes catching on each of the hairs in his eyebrows, following the lines that bracketed his mouth. The shadow of stubble on his jaw. She had watched him as the sun had crept over the horizon behind him, until he'd taken a deep breath, stretched and turned towards the window, and she'd slipped out of bed with her heart racing, terrified that she was going to be caught looking at him as if…as if she cared.

That he was going to know how she had felt about him, even if it had been only for a moment, before she had tamped down those dangerously tempting feelings.

She was simply going to concentrate on her work. She had an important meeting with Claude Gaspard, and she was not going to allow herself to be distracted by a boy just because she'd decided to let someone kiss her gently, for a change.

A change. That was the only reason why she felt a little different this morning than she had after previous sleepovers. Just because something felt different didn't mean that it was something to be afraid of. So why did she feel so unsettled? So tempted to push her work to one side and follow Adam into his bedroom, into the shower she could hear running in his bathroom.

No. This meeting had to go well. It would go well. She would return to London with a space for her fragrance in Claude Gaspard's schedule for that year and she would be triumphant, having done what she knew that Adam could not, that no one in her family could, and be the one who would rescue Kinley from its state of chronic cash-flow problems. That was what she wanted for her life. To make her career a success. To show her family that she did have value. That she was worth sticking around for.

Her parents wouldn't care. If they did, they wouldn't be on the other side of the world now. They didn't care about Kinley and they didn't care about her, and they would feel the same way whether she was a success or not. It was utterly pathetic that she cared about proving herself. She had spent most of her adult life trying to protect herself from other people's opinions but still found herself vulnerable to them. It was why she still had to take a deep breath and pull on all her armour every time Jonathan called her into his office, sure before he started speaking that he was about to tell her how disappointed he was in her. Each time it didn't happen—each time he thanked her for her work, praised her for a suggestion—she felt her guards weaken slightly, a chink of belief shining through them that perhaps she had judged him too quickly. That not everyone would treat her as carelessly as her parents had. That perhaps she'd been unfair to her brother all this time.

She glanced at the clock in the corner of her screen and started to gather up her papers. Tucking them into a folder and into her bag. She knew it all. There wasn't anything else she could do now other than hope that Gaspard shared her views on how completely well suited their two companies were and agreed to work together.

Adam walked out of his bedroom in a suit, his hair parted and slicked into neatness. She let her gaze glance off him, because he was too beautiful to look at directly. She felt something lurch in her chest.

When had he upgraded to beautiful? That word just felt so…meaningful. As if there were feelings behind it or something. As soon as they were done with this meeting, she was downgrading him back to 'hot'. Maybe that way she could look directly at him again.

'I just need to throw my things in my case,' she said, 'and then I'm ready to go.'

'Great,' Adam replied. 'If, er, you find my clothes. I…'

'Right, yeah.' She felt her cheeks heat. 'I'll go and grab them.'

'Thanks. Do we, um, need to talk…about anything?'

Something lurched. 'Why would we need to talk?' she asked with feigned ignorance. 'This was nothing, right?'

At her words, he looked equal parts re-lieved, and as if he had been punched in the stomach. It was comforting to see him unsettled, as she felt similarly.

'Right. Nothing. And when we get back to London?'

She tried to think about what she wanted. What it was safe to have. She shrugged, as if the answer didn't mean much to her. 'We can carry on like this, if you want,' she said carefully. 'No strings.' He nodded. Apparently considering it. 'As long as no one knows about it. I'm already combining work and family.'

'Sex and work and people knowing is too much,'

'Precisely. If no one else knows about it, I can pretend it's not happening and that makes everyone's lives simpler.'

'It doesn't exist outside the bedroom. Got it.' And suddenly, he was looking at her with heat in his eyes. 'Does a hotel suite count as a bedroom?' he asked.

She shook her head, slowly. 'No. This is definitely a living room.' She glanced at the table. 'A dining room at a push.' She allowed herself a moment of smug enjoyment at his disappointment. 'But if you followed me to retrieve your clothes, we would find ourselves in a bedroom.'

* * *

Livia collapsed into the airline seat with an exhausted sigh. She'd done it. Despite Claude's adamant conviction that he could not accommodate them, she'd shown him how good her plan was. The prestige—and cold, hard cash—that it would bring them both if he could meet her deadlines. And he'd agreed. He'd agreed.

She listened, her eyes still closed, as Adam lifted his bag into the overhead locker and then sat beside her. Bless him for upgrading their tickets. She had no intention of living up to 'poor little rich girl' stereotypes. She would have flown economy without complaint if he'd not done it. But now she was here, with space to think and bask in her victory, she couldn't be mad at him for arranging it.

'We should have champagne, to celebrate,' Adam said beside her, and she smiled and turned to look at him.

'We'll make a toff of you yet.'

'Well, even us plebs know the theory. I'm serious, though. We should. Celebrate, I mean.'

She smirked at him. 'I know how I want

to celebrate, and it's not with champagne.' She grinned, and looked around them.

'Here? It's not a little…public for you?'

She blushed. 'I think I can make it back to London. You're not that irresistible.'

'In London you live with your family. Who we're hiding this from. How's that going to work?'

Liv frowned and turned to him.

'I hadn't thought about that. I think you need to find a place to stay. Quickly.'

'I'm not arguing with that. But won't your brother be suspicious if I decide I suddenly need to leave?'

'I'll be really mean to you. Make it realistic that you don't want to be there any more?'

He laughed and twisted in his seat to face her, his body language mirroring hers. 'I think I like it more now you're being nice to me.'

'Pfft, I've not been nice to you.'

He frowned, though it was distinctly mocking. 'Last night felt pretty nice. This morning too. If that was you being mean, then I think we definitely can't do that in front of your brothers.'

'It was nice,' Liv conceded. 'But I wasn't being nice to you. That was all for my own benefit.'

'Oh, really?' Adam asked, raising his eyebrows. 'Even when you—?'

Liv slapped her hand over his mouth and glanced around to check that no one was listening. When she met Adam's gaze, it was full of mischief, and he nipped at one of her fingers as she drew her hand away. Adam caught her wrist and pressed a kiss there. Then to the base of her thumb, and the tips of her fingers.

'We'll find a way,' he promised. 'We can be sneaky. It'll be fun.'

She smiled back. 'Okay. We'll find a way.' She turned to face forwards, but let her head fall to the side, resting on Adam's shoulder as the plane taxied down the runway. Once they were back in London, they would have to hide this. It was the right thing to do—the sensible thing.

It would stop these hook-ups slipping into something like a relationship. But while they were thirty thousand feet in the air, she could afford to be a little soft. To soak this up. So she smiled to herself. Nothing that happened over international waters could possibly count. So she allowed herself an indulgence that she'd usually cringe away from. She slipped her hand into his, let their fingers tangle, and leaned into his side while she caught up on some sleep. For some reason—it couldn't possibly be the hours-long marathon they'd indulged in the night before, could it?—she was absolutely shattered. She didn't even complain when Adam rested his cheek on the top of her head and pressed a gentle kiss to her hair.

But when she woke from her nap, her body still warm and comfortable tucked in against Adam's side, she knew that their time out had to come to an end. She sat up and stretched as the plane touched down onto the runway. Adam blinked awake beside her. So she'd worn him out too. She suppressed a smug smile.

Liv used her key to let them both into the town house, and they shared a conspiratorial look before she opened the door. Game faces on. She absolutely did not want her brother knowing what was going on with her and Adam. Other people seeing it would mean that she might have to look at it head-on, and if she did that, she wasn't sure that she would be comfortable with what she would see.

'You okay?' Adam asked, and she faked a smile and opened the door.

''Course I am. Why wouldn't I be?' She'd thought that she'd nailed a breezy tone, but a glance at Adam's face made her wonder. She walked into the hallway, noting the quiet, other than the clip of their shoes on the check-patterned marble of the entrance hall. 'Anyone home?' she called out, only to be met with silence.

'Empty house,' Adam observed in a neutral voice.

'Don't get any ideas,' Liv said, and he held up his hands, all innocence. 'I need to get to the office and tell Jonathan that we've got the go-ahead from Claude, and then brief the team that we're now working to our tightest projected deadline.'

Adam nodded, his posture just a little more upright than it had been a moment before. 'I'll drop the bags upstairs, then you bring the car round and we'll go in together.'

Two hours later, Liv had brought Jonathan

up to date, taken a meeting with her team to prepare them for the fact that their schedule had just got incredibly tight, and then she'd started on her to-do list—which soon ran to several pages—of everything that they would have to do in order to launch their fragrance in the ideal window. She stared at the project-management software on her screen, moving different tasks, different teams, different deliverables, until she had every last task assigned and jigsawed together.

She was starting to wonder if she'd made a huge mistake pulling their whole schedule forward by a year, when there was a knock on her door. She looked up to find Adam standing there, silhouetted slightly by the florescent lights behind him. When had it got so dark in here?

He leaned into the room and flicked on the lights. 'It's late,' he said. 'Are you going home tonight?'

She stretched up, cringed at the crunching sounds that came from her spine and sighed. 'I've got so much to do.'

'More than you can finish tonight,' he pointed out. 'It'll still be there in the morning. You've barely slept in days.'

'And whose fault is that?' Liv mumbled under her breath.

'Sorry, what was that?' Adam asked, and she glared at him, because he had heard her perfectly well.

'Okay, fine. I'll go home and work there if it'll stop you nagging me. Is Jonathan going back with us?'

'He left an hour ago.'

Liv huffed. 'Part-timer. Honestly, since he and Rowan got together he's actually developed a work-life balance. I don't know what's got into him.'

'You sound jealous,' Adam mused.

'I love Rowan, but not in that way,' Liv said, deflecting the question. She unplugged her laptop and shoved it into her bag along with her phone and a travel mug.

'You know what I mean.'

She shook her head. 'I could have a work-life balance if I wanted one. I prefer a work-work balance.'

Adam took a couple of steps closer, and fixed her with an uncomfortably knowing look. 'You've said yourself Jonathan is happier,' he observed. 'Are you sure you don't want something like that for yourself?'

Liv shuddered. It wasn't as if it were really up to her anyway. Even if she decided she did want what Jonathan and Rowan had, she couldn't have it. She'd been abandoned once in her life, and she really wasn't on board with giving someone the chance to do it again.

'I like my life how it is,' she told him sharply. 'I don't appreciate being told that I'm not capable of knowing what I want. If you've decided you want something else, I'm afraid you'll have to—'

Adam stopped her with a hand on her jaw, turning her face up to his.

'Hey, stop spiralling,' he said gently. 'I want *this*. What we agreed on. That's all.'

'Good,' she said, glancing at the door and pressing a kiss against his mouth. 'This doesn't give you a say in my life, okay? I'm not being a bitch. I'm just making sure you know what my boundaries are.'

'I've got it. Now, are we going home?'

He shouldn't have used the word home, Adam told himself. Liv's house wasn't his home. He could never live somewhere like this. Somewhere so…extravagant. It was just a figure of speech. He'd lived in a hundred different places in his life, and the only place remotely like this had been divided into one- or two-room flats decades ago. He didn't belong here. He needed to remember that. Liv was right, he needed to find somewhere else to live. The thought fired up a long-suppressed fear, and he took a few deep breaths to steady himself, remind himself that he had a roof over his head tonight and enough money in the bank that he would never, ever have to sleep rough.

He glanced at the bathroom door, remembering that it connected with Liv's. If he wanted to shut out bad memories, there were worse ways to do that than to make new ones. They'd sworn to keep this a secret, that her family and her friend wouldn't find out that they were sleeping together. But they could be careful. They could be quiet. The house had been silent when they arrived home. Everyone was either out or already in bed. He didn't need to overthink this. They were casually hooking up, that was all. He opened the door before his brain demanded that he reconsider.

He scratched quietly at Liv's door, which

opened in front of him before he had a chance to change his mind. Liv was wearing a nightdress that reached the top of her thighs and had fallen off one shoulder. He clenched his fist to stop himself reaching out and fixing it.

'Hey,' she whispered, but didn't move aside to let him through.

'Hey.' He stuck his hands into his pockets, leaned against the doorframe.

'Do you want to come in?' she asked, which was everything Adam wanted to hear. But there was something not right, and he didn't know what it was.

'Is that what you want?' he asked.

Liv shrugged. 'It is. I want you. I want to have sex with you. But it feels different here. Weird.' Liv leaned on the doorframe too, and he figured they were having this conversation here, half in and half out of a shared bathroom.

'You don't bring guys home?' he asked.

She shrugged again. 'Of course I do. I don't know why I'm freaking out.'

He smiled, a little indulgent, before he caught himself. He pushed himself off the doorframe and framed her face in his hands.

Because he could see exactly why she felt weird. 'You're exhausted, babe,' he said, tucking her hair behind her ears and then turning her around with a hand on her shoulders and steering her over towards the bed. He pulled back the duvet and Liv climbed in with a contented groan. He bent to kiss her on the cheek, and she caught him with a hand on the back of his neck before he pulled away.

'Where are you going?'

'To bed. My own bed. You need to sleep.'

'Mmm…' she agreed, unable to stifle a yawn. 'But stay anyway. I just need a power nap.'

He laughed. 'You've got such a one-track mind,' he told her. Liv muttered her agreement, pulled him down on the bed by the waistband of his boxers, then rolled over and went to sleep. Adam hesitated. He hadn't planned on sleeping in her room. It seemed like asking to get caught. But Liv had pulled him into her bed. Wanted him to be here when she woke so that they could… He slid under the duvet before he changed his mind.

When he woke, it was to fingers gently stroking his belly, sliding along the lines where his abs would be if he weren't all soft with sleep. He smiled to himself as Liv hugged him from behind and pressed a kiss to the back of his shoulder. 'I slept,' she whispered into his skin, into the dark. 'I'm feeling much better now. Not weird at all.'

He chuckled under his breath.

'I can feel that.'

'Are you awake?' she asked. He laughed, turned over and pulled Liv into him.

'I am now. You know that you're not subtle, don't you?' he whispered into her ear.

'Good. Being subtle doesn't get me what I want.'

He rolled above her, and she squealed in surprise. He shushed her with his fingertips against her mouth. They both watched the door, breath held in suspense, waiting to see if they had given themselves away. But when nothing broke the silence other than their own breaths, Adam let himself relax.

'Can you be quiet?' he asked Liv, who was little more than shadows and warmth beneath him in the half-light. He felt more than saw her nod. He skimmed a hand down her side, found the hem of her nightgown, thoughts of which had kept him awake long after Liv's body had gone heavy and her breathing slow. She gasped but didn't make a sound when he skimmed his fingers over the hem, ghosting over soft skin underneath, retreating when he saw Liv bite down on her lip. She arched up towards him in protest, so he lifted his weight off her, resting on his elbows. When she dropped back to the mattress, he lowered his weight back onto her.

He knew what she wanted. She wanted this hard and fast, so she didn't have to think about what she was doing. She wanted to be swept away by something greater than herself.

He wanted her present.

He wanted to feel as every kiss landed on her skin, not glancing off as they turned or tumbled. He'd seen what she was doing. Had felt the difference in Paris when he'd had her, really had her, and now he wouldn't accept anything less than her being fully present.

She let him touch her gently, and her own fingers went exploring. The lines of his stomach, each of his vertebrae, from his neck down, slowly, slowly... When she reached the small of his back, she pressed him close again, but an invitation, rather than a demand. He bit down on the inside of his cheek as he rolled his hips against her, a reward for her honesty. A reward for Liv that had sparks following the path of her fingers down his spine. He rested his forehead against hers. Fighting for control.

'Are you okay?' Liv asked, her hand cupping gently around his backside, not demanding anything, just anchoring them together. He kissed the corner of her mouth, and then full on the lips, their tongues sliding together—familiar now. Knowing how to tease a gasp or moan.

Her eyes stayed open the whole time, locked on his, and he gasped at the intimacy of it. He had demanded this of her, not realising how much it would expose him.

Could she see how much he needed this? he wondered afterwards, as they both caught their breath, breaking their gaze. Could she see how much he craved her touch, as if it was only by being pressed against her that he felt truly himself? His mind snagged on the thought. He didn't really believe that, did he?

Liv had talked about boundaries earlier. That was what he needed now, he realised.

He flinched away from Liv, eased himself out of her arms, one eye on the door. 'I should be...' he said, glancing at their interconnecting door.

'Um, yeah, of course,' Liv said, finding her nightgown by the bed and pulling it over her head, suddenly awkward.

'If I fell back asleep...' Adam began, knowing that it sounded as if he was making excuses. 'I don't want to get caught in here.'

'No, yeah, of course,' Liv said, covering herself with the duvet, tucking it right up to her armpits. Adam felt a black hole somewhere in his chest. It had no right to be there. This was casual. It was what they both wanted—it was what they had agreed.

He kissed her cheek, perfunctory now. 'I'll see you at breakfast. Catch up on your sleep, yeah? Goodnight, babe.'

CHAPTER TEN

LIV SLAMMED THE lid of the coffee pot closed and suppressed a yawn. This bad mood had absolutely no reason to have hung around for three straight days. She'd had plenty of time to catch up on her sleep and get over being irritated with Adam because he hadn't spent the night or knocked on their interconnecting door any of the nights since. Not that there was anything wrong with that. He was absolutely right not to risk them being caught.

She'd done the same thing to him in Paris. Worse, really, sneaking out before he even woke up. So why was she throwing her teaspoon into the sink, and slamming closed the lid of the bin? She spun on the spot at the sound of footsteps in the doorway. 'Adam,' she said, in what was meant to be a friendly, neutral tone, but came out somewhere between a gasp and an accusation. He glanced behind him to make sure they wouldn't be overheard.

'Good morning,' he said, with a smile that threatened to melt away her bad mood. If only he would come over and fold her into his arms, into his body, she knew that this mood would disappear. But that would be a distinctly boyfriendy move, and she didn't want to want or need that from him.

'Coffee?' she asked him, but he shook his head.

'I think I'll make tea. Do you want one?'

She raised her coffee cup and her eyebrow.

'Right, no, of course. Have you, er…got plans for today?' he asked.

Right, because it was Saturday, and week-end plans were something that most people had. Why was he asking, anyway? Were they doing small talk? As if she hadn't breathed in his moans, taking them down into her chest, where they'd mixed with her own. But this was the deal. This was what she had to do to protect herself. 'Need to go into the office' she said. 'Lots to do. You?'

He shrugged. 'I'll work this afternoon. This morning I need to find a gym to join. I've not been since I got back to London.'

'Oh, you're really going to seed,' she said, rolling her eyes, and then catching herself. That was exactly the kind of intimacy that she couldn't allow herself where they might be seen or overheard. Adam just smiled.

'There's one in the basement of the Kinley building,' she said. 'Adam should have mentioned it. If you don't want to have to spend time looking around.'

'Yeah, that'd be good,' he said. 'Do you want to go in together or—?'

'No,' Liv interrupted. 'I'm ready to go now and I don't want to rush you, so…' A weak excuse, and they both knew it. But that was fine. She didn't owe him Saturday mornings. If that was what he wanted from her, he could have stayed the other night. Locked her bedroom door and wrapped his arms around her and tucked his chin into the notch of her shoulder from behind.

She had been there for the taking, sleepy and satisfied, and he'd chosen his cold, empty bed instead. Even a casual hookup had a right to be offended at that, didn't they?

'Okay, well, I'll see you later, then?' Adam asked.

'Uh, yeah, I suppose so.'

She poured the remaining coffee from the pot into a travel mug for later and grabbed her backpack. She'd walk in. It wasn't much more than a mile away, and she could do with the space and the air.

She skipped down the front steps, glad to be away from the house and Adam, and all the confused feelings she was carrying that morning. She walked quickly, trying to outrun her thoughts. She had no reason to be angry at Adam. All he had done was abide by the boundaries that she herself had set down. No, the only person she could possibly direct this anger towards was herself. This feeling, as if she had been abandoned. As if she hadn't been enough. That wasn't about Adam's failings, it was about her own. She knew well enough where she was weak, what small slights could feel like deep, penetrating wounds.

She was usually more careful than this. She could usually calculate just how close she could get without risking aggravating those old wounds. She would recalibrate; if she gave herself some space, it would be easier to see where she had got too close.

And the next time she was with him, she'd keep herself safe.

Thank God she had so much work to distract her. She'd lose herself here for a few hours. Refuse to think about the other night. Or their night in Paris, or how warm and utterly peaceful it had been to sleep tucked into his side on the plane. That was what her body had craved, she realised. That sensation had crept into her unconscious, making itself comfortable there, so that her brain was bypassed completely. Her body just felt unsatisfied now, when his wasn't pressed against her.

She forced herself to concentrate again on the spreadsheet in front of her, trying to make the figures cooperate. Even with the cash injection that she and Caleb had given the business, using their inheritances, things were tight, and she had to keep a firm hand on the budget. If she'd had more money at her disposal she could have simply offered to pay Claude over the odds for space in his schedule. But instead she'd had to fly out there to put on the charm offensive. And that was only one item on her very long to-do list. She had to decide on production, packaging, and then actually sending it out into the world. A publicity campaign. Advertising, print and social media and…

She allowed her head to fall into her hands and rubbed at her temples. It was a big job, but not too big. She'd managed product launches before, a dozen times. But they had never been so personal before. All the different areas of her life had converged in the last months. Living and working with her family, her best friend becoming something more like a sister. And now Adam. She was sleeping and working and living with him, which in the cold light of an English Saturday morning seemed like an utterly terrible idea. All the different areas of her life were tangled together and she had nowhere to hide from her mistakes.

She needed more coffee. She grabbed her mug and walked towards the staff break room, where she'd brew a large pot, enough to keep her going for the rest of the afternoon. And then she'd think of something to do this evening, so she didn't have to go back to the house, didn't have to go back to—

'What the hell?' She crashed into a hard,

sweaty body, and had to put out a hand to steady herself. 'Adam?' she asked, not finding herself able to take her hand off his biceps, which flexed subtly beneath her fingers. It was smooth and slick with sweat, upper arms and muscled shoulders defined by a gym vest. She kept her eyes fixed safely at arm height as she traced a finger around the outline of that muscle. A shame it didn't come with a simpler package, she thought as Adam tipped her face up with his knuckles under her chin. 'Is this what passes for work wear now?' she asked, trying to keep things light.

'Anyone would think you like it,' he said with a barely suppressed smirk.

She finally looked up and met his eye. 'It's very unprofessional.'

'Are you suggesting I take it off?' he asked.

Liv smiled. This was just banter. Smutty banter, yes, but nothing more meaningful than that. She breathed a sigh of relief. She'd been freaking out for no reason. She knew how to do this. How to keep it safe.

She sniffed theatrically. 'I'm suggesting that you go for a shower,' she said, taking a step back from him. 'You smell terrible.'

Adam chuckled and stepped even closer than he had been before. 'Am I right in thinking that it would be unprofessional to ask you to join me?'

She took a sip of coffee, looking at him over the rim of the cup. 'Very unprofessional,' Liv confirmed. 'And I think we've probably pushed our luck as far as it will go on that front.'

Adam nodded. 'Later, then? At the house?' When she didn't reply straight away, she saw the doubt creep into his expression, and then the tension in his body as he realised that she wasn't jumping on his proposition. 'Or not, that's fine too, of course.'

'Let's just play it by ear. See how we feel later,' she said.

That was better. Casual hook-ups should come with no expectations. If they happened to find one another later that night, then great. She'd like that. But making plans gave people the opportunity to let her down. Spontaneous fun was better. Except… it didn't really matter what she told Adam, when she knew full well that she would be sneaking into his bed that night, if he would have her.

'All right, then,' Adam said, his hand at the back of his neck, revealing darkly haired underarms, and flexing his muscles in a very distracting manner. 'I'll see you later, then. Maybe.'

Liv dug her nails into her palm to stop herself reaching out for him, undoing all her good work.

'Yeah, maybe.'

She watched him walk down the corridor, nursing her coffee cup in hand. And then she shook her head and walked back to her desk. She had work to do. She wasn't a teenager, and if she'd wanted to spend her afternoon mooning after a boy, she could have done that at home. In bed. But she'd come into the office to work and she wasn't going to let things slide because of Adam.

She worked solidly until she was hungry, and she guessed that it must be past dinner time. She couldn't risk Adam coming to her and suggesting dinner again. Instead she texted Rowan as she gathered her things and left the building. She needed a drink and some time ignoring how complicated her life had suddenly become.

Several cocktails and not enough carbs

later, her tongue bitten so many times to prevent herself spilling something about her and Adam, she was home, more than a little bit squiffy, a smile on her face from spending so much time uninterrupted with her best friend. If Rowan had noticed black holes in their conversation that she'd stepped carefully around, she trusted that Rowan would assume that they were Jonathan-shaped, rather than relating to their new house guest.

When Rowan and Jonathan had started dating, they had mutually agreed that discussing him was a no-go for either of them, so it wasn't unusual for one or the other of them to hide their opinion on something relating to her brother. They'd mostly talked about Liv's other brother, Caleb, who had bailed the family business out of trouble the year before with some cryptocurrency investments none of them had known about. He'd always been happy with his own company, or that of a keyboard, to which his hands were semi-permanently attached. And yet, it seemed he was spending even more time than usual at his computer.

Rowan had already tackled the workaholic habits of one Kinley brother, and wanted Liv's opinion on staging an intervention with Caleb, forcing him to leave his computer for more than food and bathroom breaks.

Liv had promised to think about it. When was the last time she had seen Caleb leave the house? Maybe Rowan was right. Seemed her friend had a better idea of what this family needed than she did. She felt a tipsy rush of affection for her friend as she poured herself a glass of water, congratulating herself for excellent hangover preparation, knowing how grateful she'd be in the morning.

Next, Adam, she thought to herself with a grin. She'd turned him down earlier, not wanting to be distracted from her afternoon's work. Not wanting to commit herself to plans even for casual sex. But there was absolutely no reason not to show up at his door for a booty call. Neither of them could possibly get the wrong idea about that. She got to her bedroom, bumping her hip on the doorframe on her way. Ouch. She'd have a bruise there in the morning. She dug around in her dresser for something sexy to wear, and pulled something skimpy and lacy over her head, giggling to herself and wondering what Adam was going to say when she snuck into his room.

She tiptoed across the bathroom, the marble floor freezing on her bare feet. Then breathed a sigh of relief when the door to Adam's room opened under her hand. She hadn't realised until it opened that she'd been worried that he might have locked it.

Adam was asleep, snoring gently, moonlight coming through the blinds showing his bare back and arms, one hand under his pillow. 'Adam,' she whispered from the door, trying to arrange herself into an inviting pose. 'Adam!' she hissed a bit louder when he didn't stir.

She crept over to him, trying to be stealthy, but nearly crying out when she stubbed her toe on the corner of the bed. 'Adam,' she whispered again. She was right beside him now, could see the soft curve of his lips, gentle in sleep, when he had no cause to smirk at her. She crouched, slightly wobbly, by the side of the bed, and touched her fingers softly to his mouth, until she slipped, and whacked her forehead against his. His eyes flew open, and she planted a hand over his mouth before he could cry out in alarm. 'It's me,' she whispered, a giggle escaping her.

'Liv?' Adam asked sleepily, pushing himself up and pulling her hand from his mouth. 'What the hell are you doing?' he asked.

'Don't you recognise a booty call when you see one?' she asked, gesturing down at her scraps of black lace.

He groaned, falling back on his pillow, which was not exactly the reaction that she had been hoping for. 'It felt more like a headbutt,' he said, rubbing at his forehead, and she planted a kiss there, climbing onto the bed and into his lap.

'Liv,' he asked as she kissed his neck, settling on top of him and making herself at home. 'Babe?' he added, when she didn't answer him.

'Yes?' Her lips curled around a smile, because she didn't hate hearing him call her that.

'Are you drunk?' he asked.

Liv sat back on her heels and thought about the question. 'Yep. Definitely tipsy.' She leaned back into him but he stopped her with hands on her hips.

'I think you should go back to bed,' he said, very seriously. She pouted.

'I haven't been to bed yet.'

'Then you should.'

Heat rushed into Liv's face, as cold took the rest of her body, and she crossed her arms over her stomach, embarrassment setting in.

'Is this because I turned you down earlier? Payback?' she asked, grabbing a pillow now and holding it to her front.

Adam pushed himself up on his hands and frowned at her. 'No,' he said slowly, watching her face. 'It's because you weren't sure if you wanted to earlier, and if you've only changed your mind because you've had too much to drink, that's not exactly an enthusiastic yes.'

Liv's face flushed with heat as she climbed off the bed. Off him.

'I'm sorry. I shouldn't have woken you. I shouldn't have come,' Liv said, pillow still clutched to her front as she walked backwards towards the door.

'Liv, wait, don't run off, it's not that,' he said, half rising from bed to follow her. But she shut the door, mortified, crossed the bathroom in a hurry and back into her own room. She locked the door, and then stood staring at it. This was bad.

Not so much that he'd turned down her slightly wobbly booty call. She could live with that. She'd had brush-offs before and taken them in her stride. What was different this time was that it had hurt. It hadn't felt as if he was turning down a quick fumble. He was saying no to *her*. Pushing her away, and that had cut through her. She pulled off her lingerie and found a simple cotton T-shirt and shorts. And then she climbed into her bed and hugged the pillow to her, tight. He'd made her care, the absolute pig. He'd made her want him enough that he could hurt her and she couldn't forgive him for it.

CHAPTER ELEVEN

ADAM WOKE SLOWLY the next morning, with a twisting feeling in his gut telling him all was not well. He didn't regret turning Liv down last night; it had been the right—the only—thing he could have done in the circumstances. But he regretted the hurt that he had seen on Liv's face. It was more than just disappointment about a rejected booty call. He was sure that she had seen more in his no than he had intended, and that was even before he'd had a chance to tell her how he had spent his evening.

She'd probably have a sore head this morning, so he went downstairs and brewed a pot of strong coffee. She appeared at the kitchen door ten minutes later. Her hair was mussed, her face pale, with dark circles under her eyes. She looked as if she was in a terrible mood, in a cute sort of way, and it took a great deal of self-restraint not to pull her into his arms and kiss the top of her head. To tell her to go back to bed and he would bring her coffee and bacon sandwiches and paracetamol. But, given how they had left things last night, he couldn't assume that she'd want him acting so…friendly. No, that was not just friendly. That was *boy*-friendly.

So he kept his mouth shut and poured her a cup of coffee, and resisted the urge to run a hand over her hair when she rested her head on the table. 'That bad?' he asked, sitting at the table, resisting the urge to laugh softly.

'Worse,' she groaned. 'I'm never drinking again.'

'Yeah, right.'

She looked up at him and winced when she met his eye. 'I'm so embarrassed,' she admitted, looking quickly away.

'Don't be,' he said, knowing it wasn't enough to fix what had gone wrong between them last night. 'Honestly, Liv,' he went on, 'you've got nothing to be embarrassed about.'

She grunted, still not looking at him. So he gave in to the urge, and smoothed his hand over her hair. 'I like that you wanted me. You looked incredibly sexy, and if you hadn't been so far gone that you literally fell over and headbutted me, I wouldn't have let you out of my sight, never mind out of my bed. Okay?'

She lifted her head and rubbed a spot just above her brow, which he could see was darkening with a bruise. 'So that's what this is. I'd forgotten that part,' she mused. 'So what did you get up to last night?' she asked. 'It's not fair that you look all…not hideous.'

Adam hesitated. They had talked about this; he had no reason to be worried. This was just a casual thing. But he had seen how hurt she had been when he had pushed her away, and he didn't want to do anything else that hurt her, however good his reasons. However much she agreed with his reasons for putting space between them. And he was more sure than ever that living together was a bad idea. He was growing far too used to this. Enjoying a grouchy, hungover breakfast far more than he should do. It wouldn't take many more mornings for this to feel as if it was his real life. As if he wanted to rely on it—on Liv—being there. Not just for casual nights or snatched moments at work, but every day, stretching out ahead of him. A future together.

But he couldn't allow himself to want something that could so easily be taken away. He couldn't bear *needing* something. To risk more months, more years of wondering how to get through the day, through his work, when all he could think about was how to get the thing he wanted. Needed. Couldn't live without. He had only known Liv for a couple of weeks, and already she had him so unsettled. He had to act now, to stop this becoming something that couldn't be undone.

'Adam?' she prompted.

'I, er… I saw a couple of apartments.' This time her head snapped up. 'Staying here was only meant to be temporary,' he said, not sure which of them he was reminding.

'I know that,' Liv replied, as if he'd accused her of something. She took a deep breath, and he watched her choose her words carefully.

'Did you find somewhere you like?' she asked. He shook his head.

'Not yet.' None of them had felt like home. He wasn't sure what it was that he was looking for. Only that he hadn't found it quite yet.

'I've got a few more to see this morning,' he added, hoping that he wasn't making a mistake. 'Do you want to come with me?'

'Doesn't that defeat the object of getting some space?'

He could hardly argue with her logic. But, he told himself, there was a difference between not sleeping together and not spending any time together at all. He shrugged, trying to convince her, as he had himself, that it wouldn't mean anything. 'It's viewing a flat, not a quicky in your office,' he said baldly. 'But it's fine if you don't want to.'

'I don't have anything better to do today. And I don't love the idea of playing third wheel to Rowan and Jonathan doing the whole Sunday domestic bliss thing. Why not? What time's the first viewing?'

He glanced at his watch. 'An hour. Can you be ready?'

She groaned and nodded at the same time.

'Need me to prop you up in the shower?' he asked. It had been meant as a joke. Not a serious invitation. Yesterday, it would have been okay. Yesterday it would have been a playful remark to be taken up or ignored. That was when he realised that something had changed. If anything like that happened again, it would not be casual. He could see that in the way that she had reacted when he had rejected her. The way he had felt about her when he'd first seen her that morning. Tired and sore and vulnerable. Nothing between them was casual any more.

'I think I'll manage,' Liv said with a forced smile as she headed out of the room. She was back downstairs in an hour, looking human again, if still tired. His heart did a weird little flip again at the sight of her, and he took a couple of breaths until it stopped. This suddenly seemed like a stupid idea, and he wondered if there was a way to get out of it. But then he remembered the look on her face when he had pushed her away last night and he couldn't bring himself to hurt her again.

When had her feelings become more important than his own? It was clear that he had crossed a line somewhere along the way, and he didn't know how to get back to the other side. The best solution he could think of was to ignore it. To pretend that he didn't feel this way. Or that he hadn't noticed them. Hadn't seen them for what they were. Something that scared him. So he smiled at her, as simply as he could, and pulled his car keys from his pocket.

'Ready to go?' he asked, his voice full of false cheer that made Liv wince.

'Ready,' she said, pouring coffee into a travel mug and shoving it into her bag— truly, her capacity for caffeine was equal parts frightening and impressive.

They walked out to the car in silence, and Adam wondered if things were always going to be this awkward now. He wanted to go back. Back to before she had climbed into his bed last night. Back to before he had felt anything for her. For anyone. When he'd finally reached a time of his life when he had everything that he needed. When both he and his mother were settled and safe. And happy.

He wasn't happy this morning. He was… unsettled. And every time he looked at Liv, he knew why. Suspected what it would take to shift this pressure in his chest. And he couldn't do it. Couldn't face the idea that this change in him was permanent.

'Oh, God, looks like this is the place,' he said, as the satnav directed them into the underground parking of a sleek new tower of luxury apartments. His estate agent, a tall, sandy-haired man in chinos and a V-neck sweater, was waiting for them by a parked car, and he reached out to shake his hand as he walked up to him.

'Hi, I'm Matt,' he said, introducing himself to Liv. Adam panicked momentarily.

'This is Liv,' Adam said, knowing full well that it looked as if she were his girlfriend. 'My colleague,' he added, though that was the least she was to him. He glanced across at her, wanting to know what she had made of that description. Her slightly raised eyebrow didn't tell him much—and his glances across at her as they travelled up in the lift didn't give anything away either.

When the private elevator doors opened, he groaned. It was perfectly clear from the moment he stepped out of the lift that this place must cost ten times what he'd told Matt his budget was. How could he justify spending multiple millions on an apartment when he knew for a fact that there was a homeless shelter within half a mile of here? He was their largest donor, as well as a trustee on their board. But it seemed as if every estate agent in London had done some research, decided his budget for themselves, and had taken it upon themselves to show him every luxury bachelor penthouse inside the M25.

Liv raised her brows at him as she stepped out of the lift and spun around to face him. 'Fancy,' she observed, walking backwards into the flat a few paces, before turning round and walking across to the kitchen area of the open-plan space, running a finger along the chrome, top-of-the-range appliances. 'This'll be perfect for all the baking you do,' she said, flicking the switch on a KitchenAid.

'I could learn,' Adam said with a smile. Liv smiled back, and he felt it low down in his belly. She walked away from the kitchen and over to the window wall that looked out over the city. He followed her over, and it was only the presence of Matt in the room that stopped him wrapping his arms around her from behind. Instead, he stood as close as he was able while keeping up their pretence of being nothing more than colleagues.

'It's almost the same view as the roof at Kinley,' she murmured, and his mouth turned up in a smile.

'Well, then, that's the one thing it has going for it,' he replied with a smile, remembering the night when he had stopped fighting what he felt for her. When they'd managed to convince themselves that this was something that they could get out of their systems and then go on as normal. How stupid that seemed now, he thought. As if having Liv, being close to her, was something that could ever make him want her less, rather than more. As if, once he knew the taste of her, he could go through the rest of his life without her. Sweat prickled at his hairline and his face flushed hot as he realised how deeply in trouble he was.

'You don't like it?' she asked over her shoulder.

'I hate it,' he told her. 'Do you know how many people you could house for the price of a place like this?'

'I didn't think it was your style,' she said with a smile, turning away from the window. 'So what are we still doing here?'

She had a point, so he followed her to the door, where Matt was standing, looking hopeful.

'What do you think?' he asked.

'I think that if you add a zero to my budget again, I'll find a new agent.' The estate agent laughed. 'Well, it was worth a shot. I promise you're going to love the next place.'

They typed the postcode that Matt gave them into the car's satnav and when they pulled up in front of a house so similar to Liv's that it could have doubled for it in the movie of her life, Adam gripped the steering wheel a little harder.

'Well,' Liv said, 'this feels…familiar.'

Matt got out of his car and held his hands up to pre-empt Adam's objections. 'I know what you're going to say but it's within budget, I promise. A garden flat.'

'Okay,' Adam said, losing a little of the tension in his shoulders. 'We'll take a look, at least.'

They walked up the steps to the front door, the line of buzzers to one side the only difference from the entrance to Liv's home. The hallway was smartly kept, and a second door led into the ground-floor apartment. Most of the internal walls had been removed, to create a light, airy, open space, but Liv noticed that the fireplaces and decorative ceiling plasterwork were so similar to her own that they must have been original. The old floorboards had been stripped and sanded and polished, and the rich golden colour bounced warm light around the room. At the back of the apartment, French windows opened onto a terrace and a garden, where sunlight played on the leaves of the tall trees that screened the space from view.

Liv watched Adam, standing unmoving in the centre of the room, hands planted in his pockets.

'What do you think?' she asked, when Matt excused himself and left them alone together. 'Better than the last place, right?'

Adam nodded, but didn't lose his preoccupied expression.

'What's wrong?' she asked.

'It's a lot like your place,' he said, and, although he didn't expand on that, it was clear he didn't mean that it was a good thing.

'Well, I'm sorry I've ruined an entire style of architecture for you,' Liv said, crossing her arms.

He turned to look at her, his expression calling her out on her childish tone without him having to say a word.

'I like it,' he said, looking pained. 'And I like that it reminds me of your place, that that makes it feel like it could become home really quickly. And at the same time—'

'That scares you,' Liv finished for him. 'It would really be that bad? Falling for me?' She asked the question knowing that it wasn't fair. Knowing that if the tables were turned, the answer would be yes, it was that bad.

Adam sighed and looked at the ceiling. 'I don't know if it's too late now anyway.'

And Liv was just about to launch a tirade of questions, first and foremost being *What the hell?*, when Matt reappeared.

'I think you like it,' he said with a smile. 'Do you want to see the bedroom?'

At which point, Adam seemed to choke on fresh air and Liv felt the room swim in an entirely unhelpful way. 'I'm just going to…' she said, and bolted for the door.

Once she was outside she dropped to sit on the top step and tried to sort through her racing thoughts. What had that meant? Too late for what—to not fall for her? She scrabbled around for any other possible meaning she could ascribe to his words but came up with nothing. He was falling for her? The only saving grace from the whole thing was that he seemed as mortified to say it as she had been to hear it. Surely this had to be the end of their... Of whatever this was. If he was falling for her then it could only be a matter of time before things went sour.

But the thought of it turned her stomach. That it would be pulled away from her without warning. Without knowing that their last time would be their last time. Maybe she was jumping to conclusions, maybe he had meant something else completely. Maybe this didn't have to be over yet. They still had time. And the fact that she was hanging on so desperately to that told her everything she needed to know about how she felt about him. If Adam was in too deep, so was she. They should both be putting an end to this. It would just be a case of which of them had the guts to do it first.

She turned and looked over her shoulder as the front door opened, and Adam appeared behind her. Matt jogged down the steps with a quick goodbye, leaving them alone with their awkward atmosphere.

Adam came to sit beside her on the step.

'So?' she asked, forcing a smile in his direction.

'I've bought it,' Adam said, and her eyes widened.

'Even though it reminds you of me?'

He smiled back at her, but it was hollow. A little sad.

'Did you mean what you said?' she asked when he didn't say anything.

He leaned forward, with his elbows on his knees, then looking straight ahead, avoiding eye contact.

'Yeah,' he sighed. 'I think I did. This has turned into something I wasn't prepared for.'

Liv nodded. Took a deep breath. 'For me too.' They sat in silence for a few moments more. If they had a different sort of story, this would be the moment when their shoulders bumped, and they leaned into each other. When she might have reached for his hand, pulled it into her lap and laced their fingers together. But that was the sort of happy ending she had never expected for herself. Being open to that meant being open to being hurt, and being with Adam these past weeks had only shown her how ill-equipped she was to handle that.

She hugged her knees to her chest and wrapped her arms around them.

'This is over, isn't it.' Not a question. She couldn't feel Adam's warmth beside her. Could feel the millimetres of space between them as a chasm.

'It's probably for the best,' Adam replied. Which wasn't the same as saying he wanted it to end, but made clear that he didn't want him to fight for her either. Was that what she wanted? she had to ask herself. Or was it just her ego that made her want to persuade him to change his mind, that painted a picture of the next few days, weeks, without him in it and how quickly that had become something so difficult to countenance? She glanced across at Adam.

'I feel like at least one of us should put up a fight for this,' Liv mused.

'Is that what you want?' he asked. 'To fight? To try and make it work?'

She fixed her eyes ahead of her. 'No,' she said, taking a deep breath and deciding on brutal honesty. 'But I wish you would.'

'I don't want this to end,' Adam confessed, and it was clear from the tone of his voice that it *was* a confession. She waited, because there had to be more to that sentence. 'But I don't want to be the one who fights for it either,' he went on. 'Because I know that if we keep doing this, it's going to go wrong. You'll panic and bolt, and I'll be left needing you and not able to have you, and that will be torture. Which is why I need you to do this. I'm begging you to end this now, before either of us get hurt.'

She reached for his hand, but stopped herself before she could grasp it, to keep a hold of just part of him. 'I think I'm already going to get hurt,' she confessed. 'Breaking this off with you hurts. But it's better now than it will be later.'

Adam nodded. 'I can move in here today,' he offered, and Liv's eyes widened.

'How is that possible? What about solicitors, and surveys, and…?'

'I'm going to rent it while we take care of all that,' Adam explained, which didn't make the hard knot in her chest go away.

'So you're really that desperate to get away,' Liv mused, resting her chin on her knees, her whole body curled in on itself.

'You said for yourself it's for the best.'

Liv nodded, because of course it was for

the best, but she'd thought that she would have a little time to get used to the idea. Not that it would be happening now, this minute. She'd thought that they'd have another night at least.

'Does it have to be now?' she asked, and she tried to make sure that there wasn't a hint of desperation in her voice. Tried not to glance back at the door to his new flat, thinking about the bedroom she hadn't trusted herself to see earlier. But her eyes darted behind her, and Adam's followed, and she guessed that he knew exactly what she was thinking. He took her hand, squeezed, and she threaded her fingers through his as he pulled her up to standing and they walked together through the front door.

CHAPTER TWELVE

ADAM SMOOTHED A hand over Liv's hair as she slept on his chest, telling himself with each glide of his hand that they were doing the right thing. This had been their last hurrah. A goodbye. Except neither of them wanted this to end. They'd both recognised that, even so, there was no way for it to continue. They'd drunk each other in. He'd run his hands, his mouth, over every inch of her. Knowing it would be their last time. That he was going to cling to this memory, and he needed all the details, knew that he would want to revisit it again and again, and he wanted to be sure he had it all exactly, the taste of the skin on the inside of her elbow, the smell of the nape of her neck, where wispy hairs swirled. The curve of the base of her spine under his hands, the sound of her gasps when she fought to keep control of herself, and the deep groan when she realised it was a losing battle and she gave herself over to him.

She stirred against him, and his arms tightened around her involuntarily. He held his breath and his entire body still, hoping against hope that she'd sleep a little longer, just to delay the moment that they would have to say goodbye. She relaxed again in sleep, and he allowed himself to breathe again. Maybe he'd have another half an hour like this. An hour if they were lucky, before they had to drag themselves into wakefulness. Into real life. The light behind the blinds grew brighter, and he held Liv a little tighter, protecting her as much as he could from what was to come. There was practical stuff to work out first. Clothes, showers, coffee. None of them a simple prospect in a house furnished for estate agent showings rather than for comfort.

Then the short drive back to Liv's house. Both of them sneaking in without being caught. Because this had to be the worst time for that to happen. Having to explain themselves just at the point when there was nothing to explain any more.

He kissed the top of her head, and the next time she moved, he pulled himself out of her arms and found yesterday's jeans on the floor. A defensive measure. If he woke up naked with her one more time, that would be it. Game over. He might as well cut open his chest and pull his heart out now.

Once he was dressed, he woke Liv with a kiss to her cheek.

'Hey,' he said as she stretched. 'Probably time we were going home.' And at that moment he saw her snap awake and remember what was happening. That this was the end. He watched her wrap something invisible around herself, something that meant that he could no longer reach her.

'What time is it?' she asked, sitting up and gathering bedding around her.

'Just after seven. Enough time to get home before work'

Liv nodded, considering. She opened her mouth to say something, but then seemed to change her mind, her mouth closing with everything still unsaid.

'Can I have some privacy?' she asked. 'I need to get dressed.' Adam nodded, stepping backwards from the bed. So this was over, then, he thought, feeling as if his centre of gravity had up and disappeared completely. He waited for her on the doorstep, and when she joined him he locked the door behind them. It had been stupid to do this here. Would he ever walk into this house and not think about this night with Liv? Had he ruined his new home the first night that he owned it?

Liv turned her key in the door and prayed for a silent, empty house beyond. Her prayers were answered, and the house was mercifully quiet as she pulled her shoes off and padded through the hall in socked feet. She didn't say a word to Adam, couldn't think of what they could say to end this. In the end, neither of them said anything. Adam took the stairs up, to his bedroom presumably, and Liv the stairs down to the basement kitchen. Where Rowan was sitting at the kitchen table, two cups of coffee in front of her, a very amused expression on her face.

'And what sort of time do you call this?' her best friend asked over the rim of her mug as she pushed the other towards Liv. 'I brought you a cup of coffee since you were sleeping in so much later than usual. And what did I find? An empty bed.'

'Rowan,' Liv said, feeling her heart start to race, her hand start to shake in panic. 'I can explain.'

But Rowan went on as if she hadn't heard her. 'And when I glanced in the bathroom,' she said, 'I just happened to notice that Adam's door was open and he wasn't home either. Fancy that for a coincidence.'

Liv dropped to a chair at the table and grasped the coffee that Rowan slid right in front of her.

'Want to talk about it?' Rowan asked at the same time as she heard the front door slam above them. Which was when she felt the tears at the back of her eyes, and she rested her forehead in one hand.

'It's nothing. Or it *was* nothing. Whatever it was, it's over now anyway,' Liv said, her hands still shaking as she held tight to her coffee cup.

Rowan frowned. 'And is that what you want, love?' she asked gently.

Liv shook her head. 'I don't know if it's what either of us want. But it's the right thing to do.' The words reminded her that she had chosen this. She straightened her shoulders, telling herself that this was what she wanted. This pain wasn't something being done *to* her. That was meant to make it better. This was meant to be what she was protecting herself from. She turned to Rowan.

'What am I going to do?'

Rowan wrapped an arm around her and pulled her into a hug. 'Why don't you start from the beginning and tell me everything?'

Liv groaned, turning to bury her face in her friend's shoulder.

'I think you're going to tell me that I've been an idiot,' Liv mumbled into her dressing gown.

Rowan laughed.

'If I do, I promise it'll be in a really lovely way. I'm going to be your sister, remember. You can't get rid of me, no matter how stupid you are with extremely pretty men in leather jackets.'

The laugh that burst from Liv brought tears with it, and she was a snotty mess within seconds. It was the word 'sister' that had done it. Because she'd spent months thinking that Rowan falling in love meant that she was losing her best friend. But she had been stupid not to see before now that she was gaining so much more than she was losing. Which brought on a final wave of tears so intense that they couldn't last for more than a few minutes. She scrubbed her face clean and dry on the tea towel that Rowan handed her and finally took a sip of her coffee.

'Rowan, I think I really like him,' she said. 'And if this is what it feels like to not be with him, I don't want to do it. I don't want to choose to feel this just because I'm scared of what might be somewhere down the road.'

Rowan gave her a considering look. 'It sounds to me like you do know what you want.'

'Yeah, but what about what Adam wants, or doesn't want?'

'It sounds like he wants you to fight. I think him specifically telling you that was the giveaway.'

'Then why doesn't *he* fight?' Liv asked, though she knew his reasons perfectly well.

Rowan forced out a breath from between her teeth. 'I know talking about me and Jonathan is a bit of a no-go, but I'm speaking from experience when I say don't underestimate how much simply being stubborn and stupid can get in the way of something really good.'

Liv tilted her head and fixed Rowan with a stare. 'Are you trying to tell me that I'm as stupid and stubborn as my brother?'

Rowan smiled, a little wistfully, and Liv reminded herself not to barf. 'I'm saying that Jonathan and I came very close to not being as happy as we are, and I hate to see you unhappy. But whatever you decide to do, I'll support you.'

Liv gave a sob as the tears made a reappearance.

'What?' Rowan asked. 'What did I say?'

Liv thought about it. If she couldn't talk about her feelings with her best friend, what hope did she have of overcoming these fears she'd been carrying around for years? So she told Rowan how insecure she'd been feeling about their friendship and how scared she was of being left behind. And the tightness of the hug she received held her heart together and gave her enough confidence to go and have this talk with Adam, because whatever she'd thought she'd wanted, it couldn't be this.

Everything in her stomach and her heart and her head told her that what they'd decided was wrong. Her whole body felt as if it were fighting against her decision. The only slight hitch in her plan was evident when she went upstairs to shower, and the door to Adam's room was open, showing that he'd cleared his stuff out already. He must have thrown it all in his bag and taken it to the office with him. She sighed, pulling out her laptop and powering it up. She was running too late this morning to go into work, so she might as well work from home. It was merely a bonus that she wouldn't have to run into Adam on the day that they had broken up and he'd moved out without even shouting goodbye down the stairs as he went.

Adam stared at the clock on the wall of his office. It was only eight a.m. No reason to think that Liv wasn't coming into the office at all. But he'd thought that yesterday, and the days before that, and had started at every footstep outside his office until he'd received her emails to say that she was working from home. He wasn't sure that he could take another day of watching, waiting for just a glimpse of her. And being disappointed.

This was ridiculous. He could just call her. Email her, even, in a professional way. She'd see through it in a second. It was one of the things that scared him the most. One of the things that he loved the most. He'd been so close to asking her for... He wasn't even sure what he wanted to ask for. For her not to let him ruin this. To force him to do the thing that scared him the most. And then she hadn't come into the office. He'd been left wanting something he couldn't have, with a sore heart, and no idea what to do about it.

He heard high heels outside his office, but reminded himself that it probably wasn't her. But then he looked up, and there Liv was, framed in the doorway, her expression inscrutable.

'Hi,' he said, shaking his head at the inanity of that one syllable. She half smiled, and it was without question the most beautiful thing he had seen since they'd left the apartment that he could hardly bear to be in now.

He had been so stupid to spend the night with her there; it reminded him more of Liv than of a fresh start as he'd planned.

'Have you got a minute to talk?' she asked him, and his heart leaped.

'Yeah, of course. Here?'

'I was thinking the roof. Five minutes?'

He nodded, struck silent, hardly allowing himself to hope. Because not only was there something to say, she wanted to say it somewhere that was meaningful to them. That had to be a good sign, didn't it? He ran a hand over his hair, smoothing it down, and then stared at the clock, each of the three hundred seconds he had to wait feeling like the one where his heart might finally give out on him.

Exactly five minutes after Liv had walked out of his office, he started after her. It occurred to him as he reached for the handle of the door out onto the roof that he probably should have spent some of those five minutes thinking about what the hell he was going to say to her. But he had been so focussed on just getting here that he hadn't thought about what he would say when he did. All he knew, all he could tell Liv was that the last five minutes—the last few days—had been torture, and if she was up for anything other than being apart, whatever that looked like, then he wanted to try it. He took a final breath and opened the door.

Liv was standing at the edge of the roof, leaning up against the wall looking out over the city. The wind had caught her hair, was playing it around her shoulders. He took a deep breath because if he was going to do this, he had to be sure. He couldn't mess Liv around. Couldn't do that to her, or to himself.

'Liv,' he said, and she turned to look at him, obviously so lost in thought that she hadn't heard the door. She smiled at him, before catching it, neutralising it.

'Adam, hi,' she said. He didn't know how it could hurt so much just to hear his name on her lips. It was the lack of feeling that really punched him in the gut. He'd heard her say his name so many times since he'd met her, and never with such lack of feeling. Was that real? He wondered, had she really been able to stop feeling anything so quickly? Or was it a front to hide how affected she had been by their break-up?

'Thank you for meeting me,' she said. He couldn't believe how awkward that sounded. Was it really only a few days ago that they had been so close? When he had been inside her body, in her life, in a way that felt impossibly distant now?

But somehow they both found themselves at the little table where they'd worked that first night. Liv sat, so he copied her, but then that felt like a mistake. This lump of filigreed iron furniture between them when what he really wanted was to pull her close. It was probably better like this, he reasoned. They needed to talk, and he wasn't sure that they could do that if they had the constant distraction of sitting too close.

'I've missed you,' he blurted. It wasn't exactly what he'd meant to say, but it was true, and, from the quirk at the corner of Liv's mouth, she was happy to hear it. That emboldened him, and he spoke again. 'I've missed you, my new bed smells of you, and I think maybe we made a mistake calling quits on this.'

Liv raised an eyebrow and he had no choice but to keep talking. 'I know I…you… we, always said that this was going to be casual, and that it was the right time to put an end to things. But if the way that I've felt since we left the flat is anything to go by, I think we've made a mistake. I should have fought for this then, but I was scared. And...' He trailed off, looking at her. Because he was spilling his guts and Liv hadn't said a word. For all Liv was saying, he could be on completely the wrong track, and she'd not given him a thought since a few nights before.

Just as he was about to lose his nerve, she reached for his hand across the table. He looked up and met her eye, and that spurred him on to finish. 'So I know you had your own reasons for being afraid of this, and maybe I'm making an idiot of myself. But if you want to try being afraid together, then I'd really like that.'

For the most nerve-racking minute of his life, she didn't say a word.

'I think I'm falling for you,' Liv said, and Adam felt his eyebrows head for his hairline. He felt a jolt of adrenaline, and he wasn't sure whether it was the fear and anxiety he would have had a week ago at those words, or excitement that she might have had the same second thoughts that he had over the end of their relationship.

'Is that…something you're happy about?' Adam asked, because it was impossible to guess from the expression on her face.

Liv shrugged, which wasn't exactly a passionate declaration. 'I wish I knew,' she said, leaning forwards, forearms on the table, her hands playing distractedly with his. 'I like you. You know how much. And these last few days have been…really awful. I don't want to give up on us. But I have all this baggage, and so do you, and what if it all goes wrong anyway and it's even worse?'

He trapped her hands with both of his. Deprived of her distraction, she looked up and met his eyes. 'That's the risk,' he said, because she'd summed up what he was feeling exactly. 'That's the risk, isn't it?' he said again, squeezing her hands and pulling them closer to him. What he really wanted was to pull her into his lap, but for now, this would have to do. 'Whether we think it's worth it to fight for this. We both have to want it, and I do. I'm terrified, but I'm not ready to give up. I've never tried to make anything like this work before, but I want to. With you.

And when you get scared, I'll be there for you, or give you space, whatever you need. And when I freak out, you'll be there for me. I think that's how this usually works. Whatever scares us, we face it together.'

He saw Liv visibly shudder and her expression turned to a glare. 'But what if we don't? What if you change your mind and run off and leave me, and I'm left with all this—' she gestured up and down her body '—all these *feelings* alone? You can't promise me that you won't leave.' Her words shocked him into silence, because he realised she was completely right. He couldn't make promises like that. And even if he did, he wouldn't be able to make her believe him.

'You're right,' Adam acknowledged. 'I can't make promises like that. I'm not sure anyone could promise that. I suppose that's where trust comes in. Can you trust me?' he asked.

Liv inspected his face, as if the answer to her question would come from his face, rather than within. 'Do you trust *me*?' she asked, batting his question back at him. He thought about it seriously, because this wasn't the time to think without speaking.

But the truth didn't come from careful consideration. It came from his gut.

'Yes,' he said. 'I trust you. I trust you to be honest with me about what you want and how you're feeling. I've never even tried to make a relationship work before, so I've got no more idea how to do that than you have, but that seems like a good place to start. If we tell each other what we want and what scares us and agree to deal with it together, I'm pretty sure that's how people build a relationship.'

Liv pulled her hands away, and a yawning chasm of panic threatened to open in his chest, so he took a deep breath to try and appease it. He was just wondering if having to prompt Liv to talk about what she was afraid of meant that they were beyond saving, when she groaned, shook her head and then spoke.

'If you abandon me like my parents did, it will break me completely and I'm not sure how I could survive that.'

He nodded, because he could see how deep those wounds cut. He could only cling to the fact that she was telling him about it, rather than holding her fears close, too scared to share them with him.

'I can promise you that I'll never ghost you,' he said. 'But it's up to you whether you can take a risk on me.'

She looked thoughtful.

'I want to trust you,' she said at last. 'And I don't want another day like these last few. But I'm going to need patience. I'm going to have to practise, and you'll be my guinea pig.'

He finally shoved his chair away and came around to Liv's side of the table.

'Is that a yes?' Adam asked, hearing the hope in his own voice.

'You heard the bit where you're going to be a guinea pig and I'm probably going to mess up? A lot,' Liv checked, as if she couldn't quite believe that he'd agreed to her terms.

Adam pulled her up, bent his head so that he could look her properly in the eye. 'I heard the bit where you want to try. Where you're as mad about me as I am about you.' Because that was the important part.

Liv rolled her eyes, but he knew she didn't mean it. Knew that what he'd said was right. 'You're not too bad. I'm prepared to admit that now,' she admitted, as he turned her face up to his with a finger under her chin.

'I'm glad about that,' Adam said, feeling a rush of courage. 'Because I'm falling for you so fast that I can hardly keep up.'

Liv tightened her arms around his neck and pulled herself up to lay a hard kiss on his mouth, only pulling away when they were both breathless and inappropriately aroused for the workplace. 'What do we do about—' she waved her arms around '—all this?'

'Work?' he asked.

'Yeah, like, are we still a secret?'

Adam shrugged. 'If that's what you want,' he said carefully.

'What do you want?'

'To shout it from the rooftops,' he said honestly, after taking a deep breath. And then glanced around them, realising where they were. 'Metaphorically speaking, that is. Unless you really want me to do it.'

'God, no,' Liv said, smiling. 'Saying it just to me is good enough. And not having to keep secrets sounds good too. Better. We could start small, with telling people.'

'Your family?'

'Yes,' she said carefully. 'Though Rowan noticed we didn't come home the other night, so...'

'So maybe we could hang out at your house sometimes. That'd be good,' he said. 'I like that we have somewhere a bit more private as well though.'

Livia gave him a self-satisfied smirk. 'Did I really ruin your flat for you? In one night?'

He gave her a stern look, tightening his arms around her waist in admonishment. 'That was meant to be a bad thing.'

She kissed him gently, and then let her teeth scrape his bottom lip, less gently. 'If it got us here, then I can't be sorry about it.'

Adam grinned. 'You know, Livia, that sounded almost…romantic.' She shoved at him, but he had hold of her too tightly for it to have much effect.

'Next you'll be okay with being called my girlfriend.' Adam held his breath, not sure how Liv would react to the word. Not sure how he wanted her to react. But she merely rolled her eyes.

'Fine, whatever, I'm your girlfriend,' she said. 'But only at home, not at the office. We need to keep things professional in the workplace.'

Adam laughed, and couldn't help pointing out that the first time that they'd slept together had, in fact, been in the office.

'Yes, but that doesn't count, because I didn't like you then,' Liv reasoned.

'And now?'

Liv rolled her eyes and groaned. 'Do you really need to hear me say it?'

Adam thought about it. About what he needed. What they both needed for this to work.

'I do,' he admitted. 'I need to know you like me. I need to know that you're as deep in this as I am.'

'Ugh. Okay, I like you,' she said, her expression deadly serious, playfulness falling away. 'I more than like you. I've never felt like this about anyone before. This is really special to me. Are you happy now?'

He kissed her gently at the corner of her mouth. She was shaking slightly, and he knew what it had taken for her to trust him with that. He kissed her mouth, pulling her in tight as her lips came alive against his, opening to him, sealing the words that they had spoken. And he held her tight because he knew Liv needed it. Because it anchored him to be there for her.

'We should probably get back to work at some point,' Liv said, and Adam sighed, nodding.

'Before Jonathan comes up here looking for us?'

Liv winced. 'Yeah, that, but also—you know—biggest product launch of my career.'

'Oh, I know you've got that completely under control. I have every faith in you. But I would like to know in advance if Jonathan's going to come after me with a shotgun.'

Liv shrugged. 'I don't know. He's kind of overprotective. But he's also pretty convinced we can't do this launch without you, so I think your life is probably safe for now.'

'So I only have to worry about my manhood? That's very reassuring.'

Liv slid her arms around his neck and smiled. 'Let me worry about your manhood for now.' He laughed, pressed his forehead against hers.

'Okay, I trust you.'

CHAPTER THIRTEEN

LIV CLEARED PLATES from the table and glanced over at Rowan, Jonathan and Adam at the dinner table, chatting as if they did this sort of thing all the time. Her brother's arm was stretched out over the back of Rowan's chair, twirling the end of her ponytail around his fingers. They made this look easy, she thought, though she knew that it hadn't been. That they'd pined after each other for years before they'd taken the plunge and tried to make it work. Blissfully happy that they now were, they'd lost years by just being afraid of opening themselves up to the idea of a relationship.

She didn't want to lose years, or even months. Days, for that matter. As much as she was terrified of what it might lead to, she didn't want to look back on her life and regret the things that she hadn't done because of being afraid.

Especially not as a result of what her parents had done. She wasn't going to let them take this from her along with all the harm they had already done. She jumped slightly as Adam's arms slid around her waist from behind, still not quite used to the fact that they weren't sneaking around. 'Okay over here?' he asked, resting his chin against the side of her head. She twisted in his arms and leaned back against the sink.

She tried not to let her smile stretch too wide, because there was no reason to let him know just how head over heels she was for him. It would only go to his head and, really, the boy didn't need to be any more sure of himself.

'I was just thinking that this is nice,' she admitted, because Adam's lips on her neck tended to have that effect on her.

'I'm glad you're happy,' he said, close to her ear. 'Because I am. But not as happy as I will be when I get you back to my place later.'

Liv grinned. 'What, you don't want to sleep in a house with my whole family?'

'Oh, I wouldn't mind *sleeping*,' he said,

still quiet so that no one else could hear. 'But I wasn't planning on letting you get much rest.' She laughed and swatted at him with a tea towel and from the corner of her eye noticed Caleb getting up from the table.

'Where are you off to?' she asked her little brother, turning away from Adam. 'Have another glass of wine.'

Caleb rolled his eyes. 'And watch you four play double footsies under the table? Thanks, but no, thanks.'

She pushed Adam away a fraction, fixing Caleb with a look.

'I'm sorry. Stay, we'll behave. All of us.' From the corner of her eye, she saw Jonathan pull his arm away from the back of Rowan's chair and lean his elbows on the table.

'Come on, Cal. One more.'

He hesitated, but then shook his head. 'Sorry, guys, there's someone I need to speak to.'

Liv narrowed her eyes as they all listened to his footsteps on the stairs.

'"Someone I need to speak to"?' Liv said. 'Do you think he's holding out on us?'

'I don't know. He barely leaves the house. If he's got someone…'

'Hmmm,' Liv said.

'Maybe let's give him some privacy if that's what the man wants,' Jonathan suggested.

Jonathan's hand had found the nape of Rowan's neck again, and Liv averted her eyes, and then turned away from the table completely.

'Ready to head off?' Adam asked, and Liv smiled, wondering whether the mind-reading was a sex thing, a spending-all-their-time-together thing, or a love thing. She stopped herself in her tracks with the word. *Love?* She looked at it in her head for a long time, waiting for the fear, or panic, or need to scarper to set in. But it just... didn't. The word sat there, comfortably, securely, and waited for her to wrap her head around it.

'Ready,' she said, looking up at him, wondering whether it was too soon to say it out loud.

'I don't know why you even bother with separate places,' Jonathan said idly, his eyes fixed on Rowan. 'You've not spent a night apart in weeks.' He looked up abruptly then, and Liv suspected that he'd first received a quick kick under the table. 'Oh, not that it's any of my business, of course,' he added hastily.

Rowan and Liv rolled their eyes in unison.

'Right, let's go,' Liv said, grabbing Adam's hand and heading for the stairs before her brother could make things any worse.

'He's right, you know,' Adam said as they reached the street. 'You've been at my place every night for—what—two weeks? Three?'

Liv stiffened. Was this where the other shoe dropped? Had it all been so good between them that she'd missed that it had been *too* good?

'Stop panicking,' Adam said, wrapping an arm around her shoulders, pulling her in tight and kissing the top of her head. 'I mean it. I know what you're thinking. I like having you here, but Jonathan's got a point. We don't need two places if we're going to spend every night together.'

Liv stalled.

'And maybe you should warn a girl before you spring something like that on her.'

Adam laughed nervously. 'Is that a no?'

'I'm sorry, did you ask a question?'

Adam sighed, but she'd not made this easy for him before, so why should she start now?

'You're really going to make me ask?'

She crossed her arms, not budging.

'Fine,' he said, his face as implacable as hers. 'Liv, will you move in with me?'

'Not if you're not even going to ask me nicely.'

He pulled her to him, wrapping his arms around her. 'Darling.' She laughed at the ridiculous endearment that he'd never used before. 'Liv, babe—'

'Better...'

'Babe. My flat only feels like home when you're in it, and I hate the thought of sleeping in my bed without you there, and I want to make you your first cup of coffee every morning. Will you please move in with me? Satisfied, now?'

He let go of her and crossed his arms, mirroring her body language. But she knew that he wasn't really cross. That he was just giving her the space to think this through without her having the pressure of knowing how much he wanted it.

'Fine,' she said at last, making sure it sounded as if she would be doing him a favour. 'I'll move in with you. I might as well now I've fallen in love with you.' She watched her words hit, slightly amused at how his jaw dropped.

'That's not fair,' Adam said, and she raised a questioning eyebrow. 'I was going to say it first,' he went on. 'And now you've stolen my moment.'

'Can't have you getting too comfortable,' Liv said with a smug smile, the knowledge that he loved her spreading from her chest out to the tingling tips of her fingers. She tucked them into the front pocket of his jeans, using them to pull him closer. 'I'm sorry,' she said, not feeling it in the slightest. 'You can say it now, if you want,' she offered.

'Oh, can I?' Adam asked, sarcastic. 'I was thinking maybe I'll wait. Tell you in my own time.'

Liv smiled. Because she didn't need him to say it. She could see it in his expression. Could feel it every time she was with him. He could say the words in his own time if that was what he wanted. She was in no hurry. They had so much time ahead of them, and she could wait, if it was for him.

EPILOGUE

'IS THIS EVERYTHING?' Adam asked, as they carried the last two boxes up into the flat and left them piled by the fireplace.

'I think so,' Liv said, wiping sweat from her forehead and looking around at the chaos. 'Rowan'll text me if any of my stuff got mixed with hers.'

After six months of all living together, she'd decided to rent out her house. Rowan and Jonathan had already been looking for somewhere, and she was never there anyway. When she'd asked Caleb about it he'd merely shrugged, and said that he'd find somewhere.

She'd have to decide what she wanted to do with her inheritance. She could invest the cash in the business. But Kinley's cash-flow problems were further and further behind them and she had bigger ideas than that. Like the homeless shelter around the corner from the town house. She just needed the right moment to talk to Adam about it. A meeting with the trustees of the charity to find out whether a cash donation or the property itself would make the biggest difference to their work.

She could face the idea of selling it, because the idea of change no longer seemed so terrifyingly destabilising. The last few months had brought more changes in her life in any period since her parents had left her without a backward glance, and she was happier than she'd ever been.

It wasn't that she had Adam now—though it was certainly no chore to be woken by his kisses on the back of her neck, his hands on her waist. It was that she had chosen to trust him, and herself, and the future.

'You know, I love…this colour on you,' Adam said, pulling at her dusty, sweaty T-shirt, which had once been white, but was now a delightful shade of dishwater grey. It had become a standing joke between them that he hadn't yet said the words. Liv didn't really mind. She knew that he felt them. And it had been enough of an adjustment to hear *herself* saying the words. More than once, since that first time. But for the first time, she felt a little twinge at not hearing them back. They were living together now, after all.

'Hey,' Adam said, catching her face between his palms, turning it up so that she'd have no choice but to look at him. 'I love you,' he said, desperately serious. She felt the smile break across her face.

'Of course you do,' she replied. 'Why wouldn't you?' Adam laughed, and then kissed her so thoroughly that she could be in no doubt about how he felt about her.

'A lot,' Adam added. 'I love you a lot. Making you so mad at me that you wanted to kiss me into being quiet is the best business decision I have ever made.'

She pushed at his chest, knowing his arms were tight enough around her waist. That he wouldn't let her go.

'I love you a lot too,' she said quietly. 'I can't imagine the rest of my life without you in it,' she confessed, pushing her hands into his chest to stop them shaking.

'Good,' he said, wrapping his hands around hers, pulling them up to press his

lips against them. 'Because I'm not planning on going anywhere.'

Liv sniffed, and he rubbed under her eye
with a thumb. 'You'll tell me when I'm allowed to ask, won't you?' he said quietly.

Liv gave him a questioning look, confused. 'Allowed to ask what?'

Adam smiled, but didn't answer her question. 'Let me know when you've worked it
out, and I'll know it's the right time.'

She nodded, a little dazed, having just
worked out what question he meant, and
wondering how mad he would get if she
asked him to marry her first.

* * * * *